NIGHT TERRORS

JIM MURPHY

SCHOLASTIC
HARDCOVER

Scholastic Inc.
New York

Library of Congress Cataloging-in-Publication Data

Murphy, Jim, 1947–
Night terrors / by Jim Murphy.
p.   cm.
Summary: A chatty old gravedigger shares chilling tales he's heard in his
wanderings from one cemetery to another.

ISBN 0-590-45341-6

1. Ghost stories, American.   2. Children's stories, American.
[1. Ghosts — Fiction.   2. Supernatural — Fiction.   3. Short stories.]
I. Title.
PZ7.M9535Ni   1993
[Fic]—dc20   92-27102
                                                            CIP
                                                            AC

12 11 10 9 8 7 6 5 4 3 2   5 6 7 8/9

Printed in the U.S.A.   37

For Ellen and Bob — sweet dreams

CONTENTS

NIGHT TERRORS

▲ 1 ▲
DIGGER'S PROMISE

I know what you're thinking. You're thinking, "What can this old geek know about anything?" Well, you're right about me being old. Older than dirt. But don't be fooled by the sagging skin, or the hair in my ears, or the way my hands quiver. That's this worthless body of mine giving up, not me. Not my mind anyway. My mind is as clear as it was sixty-three years ago when I got my first job digging graves.

That was in New York State in a tiny place on the Hudson River called Garrison and I was fourteen. You add up the years and you'll know why my body has had it. I was paid fifty cents to help a man named Clement Arnold dig a hole four feet wide, eight feet long, and six feet deep.

You're laughing at the fifty cents, I'll bet. You think I got gypped. But back then fifty cents was reasonable money, almost as much as my father was making at the lumber mill for a day's hard labor. Besides, the Great Depression was in full swing then, so any amount of money looked good to me. I went back the next day and dug another hole. And then another and another. People are dying all the time and just about every one of them needs a hole to be buried in, so there was plenty of work for me, even when times were bad.

Anyway, come winter and the ground froze up solid. It was so hard that our shovels barely dug a chip of dirt out no matter how much we pushed. Pretty soon we had to go to picks and chisels and sledgehammers, but even then we got behind schedule since the colder it got the more people seemed to die. So Clement decided to use dynamite to blast out holes.

Clement seemed like a smart man; at least he was always telling stories about the strange stuff that happens in cemeteries and saying smart things like, "You kids are in too much of a hurry these days. Always rushing around and never standing still long enough to learn a decent trade. All you have to do is use your head a little, slow down enough to listen, put some sweat in, and in no time you'll be a first-rate digger." Using dynamite seemed like a smart idea, too.

Only I guess Clement wasn't paying much attention that day. It might have been the icy wind that distracted him. Or his cold. He'd been sniffling something bad for three days. I guess it could have even been the story he was trying to tell me about the biggest person he'd ever had to bury. Whatever, Clement put three sticks of dynamite in a tiny hole we'd managed to dig, lit the fuse, and stood up.

"He was a huge man. Must have weighed eight hundred pounds," I heard Clement say. He was studying the burning fuse carefully to make sure it didn't go out, so his voice sounded far away and faint. "Maybe even a thousand. Imagine weighing that much. Needed a coffin twice as wide as a regular one and almost twice as high. You should have seen it. Had to rent a crane to get it in the hole. Anyway, guess what this fat man's nickname was? Go ahead, guess."

I had already gotten behind a gravestone some seventy feet away and was waiting for Clement. "No idea," I shouted back, peeking over the top of the gravestone. "What?"

"You won't believe it. Not in a million years."

All of a sudden Clement got this strange look on his face. It was like he couldn't remember the end to the story. Or maybe he was about to sneeze. Doesn't matter much now. The next second that dynamite went off with a roar that ripped up the frozen earth, a couple of graves nearby, an old apple tree — and Clement.

That's how I got the scar above my left eye. A chunk of dirt as hard as a rock hit me there and knocked me cold. I don't think that's what Clement meant when he told me to use my head, but I've been thankful ever since that I had a head hard enough to take a direct hit like that.

A couple of days later Clement was buried in the last hole he'd dug, which was kind of fitting if you think about it. That same day, the owner of the cemetery raised my pay to fifteen dollars a week and put me in charge of the digging. Not bad for a fourteen-year-old.

It wasn't long before I hired a kid who was thirteen to help me and I managed to follow Clement's advice about using my head, too. See, whenever we had to use dynamite I had the kid light the fuse while I waited behind a gravestone. He didn't seem to mind and, anyway, I gave him an extra ten cents each time so he made out okay. And I never bent the kid's ear with lots of foolish advice, other than to suggest he get as far away from the dynamite as possible.

I did miss Clement's stories, though. Missed 'em a lot. They filled up the air and helped pass the day. The kid I hired didn't have any stories, at least none worth repeating. I only had the few Clement was able to tell me before the explosion, and I found I couldn't spin them myself. Not as good as Clement. So I started listening hard to the others who work the cemetery — the undertakers, the livery drivers, temporary diggers. Wrote them down just like they were told, though I kind of update them every time I tell 'em so they don't sound funny. In fact, I couldn't tell you which ones I heard yesterday and which ones I heard thirty years ago, but then again, I'm not writing a history book, so who cares?

You aren't going to find any advice or warnings in these stories, either. I won't even tell you that they're all true. You probably wouldn't believe anything anybody as old as me tells you, so why waste my breath, right? I will say that if you hang around cemeteries long enough you hear about a lot of strange things and some of them are worth repeating. Like this first story. Fellow helping to dig a hole told it to me not more than three weeks ago, so you can say it's real fresh. But you should make up your own mind about it and that's all I'll say, except that if you want you can call me Digger. Oh, yeah, about that thousand-pound fat man's nickname. I asked around, but nobody had ever heard about him or his giant coffin. I guess you could say that when Clement blew up, he blew the punch line, too.

JUST SAY YES

K elly inched down the long, dark hallway as quietly as she could. Right behind her, and worrying every inch of the way, was her best friend Marissa.

"I'm not sure we should be doing this, Kelly." When Marissa was nervous, she had a habit of talking very quickly, running words together as if her life depended on getting as much said in as little time as possible. Today she seemed to be especially jittery. "It's really hot in here. And creepy with the lights out and nobody around. And my head feels like it's going to explode. Do you have any aspirin?"

"Shhhh," Kelly hissed as she drew near the corner. She should have guessed that Marissa would try to weasel out. She's the one who always has these wild schemes, Kelly thought, and then backs down at the last minute. Well, not this time. Not with Brian counting on me.

Kelly slowed her steps and leaned forward to peer down the intersecting hall. No lights were on in any of the classrooms, no talking could be heard. The second floor of Benjamin Franklin High was as still and as lifeless as a cemetery at midnight and yet Kelly sensed a presence, as if someone were watching.

"I'm not kidding. We could get into trouble for this," Marissa mumbled. "We could get kicked out of school. We could . . ." That was when Marissa slammed into Kelly and sent her sprawling on the floor with a thud.

"Marissa!" Kelly was as close to shouting as she could get without actually raising her voice above a whisper. "Watch where you're going, will you?"

"Sorry," Marissa said. She inhaled to calm herself, then helped Kelly get up. "I guess I'm scared." Suddenly, Marissa had that little lost kid look that Kelly remembered from grammar school, the one that asked for comfort and help. She felt herself giving in, feeling sorry for Marissa. We really could get into trouble, Kelly told herself, then banished the thought from her mind. What was it their gym teacher was always telling them: No pain, no gain. And she had a lot to gain by getting the exam.

"You were plenty healthy when you volunteered us in front of all those kids," Kelly said.

"I know, I know." Marissa shook her head a few times, drew in a gulp of oxygen, then searched the shadows as if they were alive. "But that was in the cafeteria. I didn't think it would be like this. It even *smells* funny now. It smells like . . . like . . ." Her voice dropped to the merest whisper. "It smells like death."

"That's formaldehyde. From Mr. Giambroni's room," Kelly sighed. "You remember him, don't you? That's why we're here. Now come on" — she took hold of Marissa's wrist and led her down the hall toward the door of the biology lab — "we don't have much time."

"You don't have to go through with it, you know." Marissa's voice was calmer and slower now. "I'll tell everybody I chickened out . . . that I puked on the stairs. Brian'll believe that. He won't think *you* were afraid or anything."

"It's too late to back out," Kelly said, tightening her grip on her friend's arm. Kelly had wanted to get Brian's attention for several months, since his first day at Ben Franklin, really, and she wasn't about to mess things up now. "You got me into this and you're going to help me get that exam, understand?"

Kelly focused her attention on the locked door. I just hope I don't mess up, she thought. How did she ever let Marissa volunteer her to steal a copy of Giambroni's midterm exam anyway? Then she remembered Brian's blue eyes and the way they seemed to ask her for help.

She and Marissa had been searching for a table in the crowded cafeteria when Marissa spotted some kids she knew. When they got there everyone was talking about the upcoming exam, only Kelly didn't pay much attention at first. How could she? Brian was sitting there, too.

"It's a killer," a girl named Trish had said between bites of her sandwich. "Half the class fails." She swallowed, then looked toward a red-haired girl dressed entirely in black on her left. "Isn't that right, Jeannie?"

"More than half," Jeannie corrected, pushing a pair of rose-tinted glasses back on her nose. She rummaged through a black knapsack until she found a tiny piece of paper. "Fifty-seven percent, if my data about his last three classes is an accurate indication. Giambroni does it every year. On purpose. He thinks it makes everybody study harder for the rest of the semester."

"And he's never given anybody an A," Trish added. "Never."

"I don't care about getting an A. Or a B," Brian said quietly. "All I care about is passing. If I don't, I can't play football."

His voice was so soft and sad that it shocked Kelly. Brian was the team's quarterback, its leader. His voice was always strong and confident when he barked out signals. Even in school, he had a way of commanding attention and respect. This vulnerable side was something new and strangely pleasing to Kelly. It made her feel a little stronger somehow, made her want to do something to help him. That was when Marissa blurted out, "Kelly was just talking about that, weren't you? She's got a plan."

"A plan?" Brian asked. "You mean like a study plan or something so you can pass?"

"It wasn't anything, really," Kelly stammered.

"What are you talking about?" Marissa faced the circle of kids. "She wants to break into the bio lab and make a copy of the test. Giambroni keeps it in his top drawer and Kelly knows how to pick locks, right?"

"Is that true?" Jeannie asked. Even through the tinted glasses Kelly could see Jeannie blink her eyes, obviously impressed. "The odds against something like that succeeding must be amazing, in the hundred-to-one range, I'd bet. You must be pretty good."

Kelly shrugged. "I was just talking, you know, thinking out loud . . ."

"Just talking!" Marissa broke in. "Listen, Kelly's got it covered. She knows what staircase to take to avoid the janitor, how long it will take to get the door open and make a copy of the test. Twenty minutes in and out, you said."

She wanted to strangle Marissa and maybe toss her into some sewer, too. She'd only been joking about stealing the test out of nervousness, making up a plan for the fun of it. Now these kids probably thought she was a jerk.

"Really?" Brian asked. "Do you think you could get a copy? I'd do anything to see that test. Anything."

Kelly gulped. She'd never been the sort of person to act silly over a boy, especially one on the football team. But Brian had seemed different — quieter, more considerate, and thoughtful in class. The idea that she'd like to get to know him better took shape over several weeks' time, almost as if a voice inside her brain, faint and distant at first, then more insistent, was urging her on. Next, she'd found herself working up the courage to talk to Brian, to ask him out, all the time hoping he'd notice her and make the first move. Now he'd done it — though she hadn't exactly planned on breaking and entering as their first date. Even so, he looked so hopeful sitting there at the table, his sandwich untouched. Maybe she could get Brian to sneak into the lab with her and together . . .

"Of course she can do it. Kelly is great at figuring stuff out. And I'm her number one helper, right?" Marissa was so proud to be the center of attention that she put her arm around Kelly and smiled as if they were having their picture taken. "Remember you said that it would only take us two. Boom, we'd be in and out, no fuss or bother at all. Remember?"

Kelly nodded feebly. Strangling and the sewer were too good for Marissa, but she wasn't sure what punishment fit the crime of having a big mouth.

"We'd really owe you if you got it," Jeannie added, with Trish nodding in agreement.

"Especially me," Brian said, smiling, his big blue eyes looking right into hers in a way that made her shiver. He needs my help, she remembered telling herself.

That's how she found herself standing in front of the door to the bio lab. Her wild imagination, Marissa's big mouth, and Brian's blue eyes. Well, now that she was there she might as well get on with it.

"Listen for anybody on the stairs," she instructed Marissa as she pulled a metal nail file from her pocket and held her breath. If this doesn't work, I'm cooked and Brian will probably never talk to me again. Okay, hands. Time to stop shaking. He's counting on me.

She placed the flat part of the file handle against the door bolt, pushed to put pressure on it and began wiggling and walking it along the metal. Move, move, she coaxed the lock. This is how that guy did it in that cop movie, only it looked a lot easier for him. She leaned over to get a closer look, carefully working the file against the lock.

"It's moving," she said. A sixteenth of an inch at a time, but it was moving. "Come on, come on, keep moving," she muttered.

"Hurry," Marissa said. "Are you almost done?"

"Shut up."

"Don't 'shut up' me," Marissa said, giving Kelly a jab in the back. "I'm taking a big chance, you know."

"You!" Kelly stopped moving the file and looked up from her job.

"Yes, me! If I get caught my parents will kill me, and no college will want me, and my whole life will be ruined. I'll probably get tossed off the yearbook staff, too!"

"*Now* you think of that stuff," Kelly said, angry for the first time. "You never think things through, Marissa. You just open your mouth and stick your foot in it. And mine. And your parents are nothing compared to mine. If I get caught, I'll be lucky if I ever get out of the house again. Now shut up and listen." She went back to wiggling the nail file, beads of sweat forming on her upper lip.

"I'm sorry, Kelly," Marissa mumbled. She gave Kelly a conciliatory pat on the shoulder. "I thought you'd want to do it. You know, for Brian."

"It's okay," Kelly said. "I guess I'm just nervous, too. I keep feeling that someone's here, watching us . . ."

"You too?" Marissa gasped. "I felt the same thing. It's the evil eye. Mr. Giambroni's evil eye, that gold thing he wears around his neck."

Kelly wanted to say something nasty about Marissa's strange thought patterns, but didn't. She really did feel something nearby, a force that was both dark and inescapable. I've got to concentrate, I've got to be strong, she reminded herself. Brian is counting on me. Those other kids are, too. Just then the file seemed to jump in her hand, the bolt clicked and slid aside.

"It's open," Kelly whispered, grabbing the handle and yanking the door open before the bolt slid closed. "I did it. I did it. Quick" — she grabbed Marissa and hauled her into the lab — "let's get going."

The wooden door swung shut with a solid, entombing crash and immediately the two girls were surrounded by the overpowering smells of chemicals and disinfectants, pickled specimens, and cages filled with nervous, squeaking mice. The room was swelteringly hot, too, and Kelly had to fight a wave of nausea that came over her.

After a few moments, Kelly regained her bearings. "You stay here. If you see or hear anything, let me know, okay?"

"Okay," Marissa said weakly, her face pale. She watched out the window in the door while Kelly hurried to the front of the room.

There was no mystery about where the test was. Giambroni made a show of placing his tests in the top drawer of his desk, as if he were issuing a dare. Kelly slipped the point of the nail file into the lock and was surprised to feel it give way easily. I'm getting to be a regular pro at this, she thought, easing the drawer open. There it was — the midterm exam.

She took a piece of paper and a pen from her pocket and reached for the test. Giambroni had said there would be forty questions and a brief essay. With luck, she could copy it all down in ten or fifteen minutes.

Glancing briefly at the first question, her pen began racing across the paper, copying down key words and phrases. This was no time to worry about exact wording or neatness. A general notion of the question was enough. She had only gotten five or six questions copied when she heard Marissa gasp.

"What?"

Marissa was wide-eyed, her mouth open. This time she really did look ill. "Someone's coming . . . the hall door . . . I heard it open."

Kelly looked around the room frantically. Stay cool, she cautioned herself. Use your eyes and brain. Like Brian does when he's scrambling around looking for receivers. There has to be someplace to hide. Under the tables maybe. Or under his desk. How about the supply closet? That's it, the supply closet. To her relief, she saw that its door was open a crack.

"Lock that door in case it's Giambroni," she ordered, dropping the test back into the drawer and closing it securely. "Then meet me at the supply closet." Kelly raced to the back of the room to check out the closet. "Hurry up. There's room in here for both of us."

The closet seemed to suck the girls inside. Both sat on the floor, Kelly pulling the door almost shut, careful to leave it open a fraction of an inch for air. Even with the tall sliver of light, the small space was as black as any pit.

"We're going to die in here," Marissa said, pushing herself against the wall. "We're going to die and our bodies are going to rot and smell." Then she went perfectly still.

"Marissa, listen to me. We have to stay calm. We have to . . ." Her voice faltered at the sound of footsteps coming down the hall, the gait slow and deliberate. The way Mr. Giambroni walked. What did I do to deserve this, Kelly wondered.

A key was inserted in the lab door, followed by a gentle creaking as it opened. Marissa latched onto Kelly's arm and squeezed it so hard that its circulation was cut off and Kelly's fingers began to tingle. The footsteps were louder now, coming toward the closet. Kelly started to whisper a prayer when the shadow of Mr. Giambroni passed in front of the closet door and proceeded up an aisle.

She let her breath out slowly, quietly, and looked at Marissa as if to say "that was close." Her friend must have understood the look, because she nodded her head.

"My pretties," Mr. Giambroni said in a hushed, soothing voice. "I'm happy you're excited to see me."

"He knows," Marissa said as softly as possible. Kelly leaned toward the crack and saw Mr. Giambroni clearly. He was on the other side of the room, about thirty feet from the closet, and had opened one of the mice cages. A tiny white mouse sat in the palm of Giambroni's hand, and he was studying the creature intently.

"So plump, so tender," Giambroni said as he looked into the mouse's black eyes. "Don't be afraid, don't be afraid. You've had a pleasant life. No work, no worry, no cold nights. Better than most of your kind. Better than most humans, for that matter. And I'll be eternally grateful for what you're going to do for me."

What a mouse is going to do for him! He's crazy, Kelly thought. He's sniffed too much formaldehyde or something. The next second, Giambroni opened his mouth and popped the mouse in as if it were a piece of popcorn. The last thing Kelly saw was the mouse's tail wiggling as Giambroni's lips came together, and then a bulge in his throat as the creature slid down.

Kelly pulled away from the door and sat bolt upright, her stomach heaving violently, a terrible sweet-acid taste rising in her throat. She remembered the wiggling tail and had to suck in as much air as she could to keep from vomiting.

"A tasty snack, very tasty," he commented matter-of-factly. "You're next." Another cage door squeaked open and Giambroni's soothing litany of words began again. Kelly found herself rocking back and forth, trying to push the knowledge of what was about to happen from her mind. She glanced at Marissa. Even in the dark, she could tell Marissa's eyes were closed and she was rocking nervously, too.

"You're shocked, of course," Giambroni's

tone was as soft and as calm as before. "You've never seen a mouse gobbled down, especially by a teacher. I know how you must feel. I do, really."

Kelly stopped rocking and sat perfectly still. Was he talking to the mouse or had he heard Marissa?

"There's nothing to worry about, not really," Giambroni said. He sounded like a kindly old doctor talking to a frightened patient. "Nothing will happen to you, nothing that you don't ask for. Relax, relax . . ."

The calming string of words continued until there was a pause, followed by another satisfied gulp. Kelly squeezed her eyes shut, but the vision of a wiggling pink tail still haunted her. Despite her revulsion, Kelly forced herself to lean toward the opening in the door again. Giambroni hadn't moved at all. He was still staring into the mouse cages. She felt herself relax, pleased at the way they'd deceived him. A real psycho, she thought. But at least he doesn't know we're here.

"But I do know you're there, Kelly." His voice had not changed in any way, still gentle and soothing, and yet it came to Kelly like a punch in the stomach. Her pulse began racing, her breathing quickened and a creeping numbness she could not fight seized her brain until she felt completely paralyzed. "I've known all along." There was a pause and then he added, "Why do you think the locks opened so easily,

Kelly? I wanted you here, where no one will interrupt us. Nothing can escape my attention. Nothing."

Escape. The word seemed strange and without meaning when it first forced itself into her thoughts.

"Ignore it," Giambroni instructed. "It means nothing to you, believe me. Nothing."

Again the word seeped through the numbness that filled her head. Escape. Slowly its meaning took shape and, as it did, her body gained a renewed energy. She thought a second about the word, then realized the obvious. We've got to escape.

Kelly began shaking Marissa's arm violently. "Snap out of it, Marissa. Do you hear me?" Her friend did not acknowledge her in any way. "We've got to get out of here. Marissa! Please, Marissa!"

"I'm afraid she can't hear you right now," Giambroni answered. "She hears no one but me. You should be more like her, Kelly. You should listen more carefully. . . ."

No way, Kelly thought, as she rolled toward the closet door. She tried to leap to her feet, but her legs were suddenly stiff and wobbly, her arms felt as if they weighed a thousand pounds. Instead of a nimble sprint to safety, Kelly lost her balance. Her face smashed into the closet door and she tumbled out and onto the floor of the lab.

"You should be more careful," Giambroni

said, "or you might hurt yourself." After a brief pause, he added, "That's your second bad fall of the afternoon."

I'm not giving up, Kelly screamed to herself, using a chair to push herself to her feet. I'm not! The door to freedom was only twenty feet away and Giambroni had not moved to block her exit. In fact, he was still facing the cages on the other side of the room as if nothing unusual were going on. I can do it, I can beat him to the door. She commanded her legs to run but they refused to obey, refused to budge an inch. She was rooted in place like some marble statue, trapped in a world that seemed to have shifted into slow motion.

She searched the room, hoping for help, for some clue that would lead her to safety. Marissa still sat in the shadows of the closet, rocking back and forth rhythmically. No, she was definitely on her own. She opened her mouth to scream, but no sound emerged.

"It really isn't worth the effort," Giambroni said, turning to face her. His expression was exactly the same as when he taught class, relaxed, alert, mildly amused. "I am in control now."

You're crazy is what you are. She couldn't move, but her thoughts seemed as quick and as loud as ever. And sick. You're disgusting and sick!

"Disgusting? Sick? Oh, the mice." Giambroni shrugged and gave her a shy smile. "How can I explain this without seeming to be . . . well, as you say, disgusting and sick. They were my afternoon snacks, that's all. Their blood, as feeble as it is, is enough to give me a charge of energy. I can already feel the mice being digested and their blood being drawn into my system." His face took on a sudden glow of happiness. "It's a remarkable feeling, Kelly. Truly remarkable. But nothing at all like human blood. Now that is a real treat." His lips turned up in a broad smile that revealed two long, white fangs as sharp as any needle.

Mouse blood! Human blood! And those teeth! He's evil! He's a . . . a . . . the word was trapped inside her head, refusing to come out. It's too stupid, she thought. Creatures like that don't exist.

"Of course we do," Giambroni said. "I'm proof of it. I wish you could relax, Kelly. As I said before, nothing will happen to you unless you agree to it. You are safe, believe me. I've just taken the liberty to temporarily freeze and silence you so we have the time to present our case carefully. You do understand, don't you?"

No, I don't understand, you lunatic. I don't understand one bit. Then it dawned on her. He'd used the word "we." Who is we?

"Good question. Let me introduce you." With this, Giambroni snapped his fingers and the lab door swung open to reveal Trish and Jeannie. "They thought you might like to join. We're looking for someone just like you. Strong-willed, imaginative, a quick thinker. . . ."

I just met them. They don't know me. They don't even know my last name, I'll bet. How could they think . . .

"Oh, it wasn't just Trish and Jeannie who suggested you," Mr. Giambroni said, nodding toward the supply closet. "Your friend did, too."

My friend? Marissa? But she's scared silly. She's . . . When Kelly turned she found Marissa standing next to her.

You! You're one of them! I can't believe it. Why didn't you say something? Why didn't you tell me?

"Tell you?" Marissa said. "Tell you what? That I hunt small creatures at night as a quick energy snack. That once in a while I'll find a human and drain a pint or so." She opened her mouth to show Kelly her fangs. "Even if I'd shown you these, it wouldn't have mattered. You would have had me packed off to the funny farm in a second."

This can't be true. My best friend. Trish and Jeannie. Even one of my teachers. She looked at Marissa. You were afraid out in the hall, you stammered and everything.

Marissa beamed with pleasure, as if Kelly had just handed her an Academy Award. "Mr. Giambroni said I had a flair for the theatrical, that I could become a famous actress someday. I was just practicing on you to see if you'd believe me. Besides, if I hadn't acted afraid, you would have suspected something, right? And then you might not have come into the lab. I'm not afraid of anything, really. Or anyone. That's one of the benefits of joining, Kelly. No more fear, no worry. Ever. It's amazing."

"It's more than amazing, Kelly," Trish added enthusiastically. "It's a blast. You can read people's minds, which makes answering stupid test questions really easy. And you can do all sorts of other neat stuff, like freezing people in place. I'm new at it and it takes practice, you know. I haven't really mastered it yet, but I'm getting better. Yesterday, I got a squirrel to stand still for almost fifteen minutes."

"My zits went away, too," Jeannie added. "Mr. Giambroni said it had something to do with the way molecules react when blood types are mixed."

Great, Kelly thought. The secret of a beautiful complexion is to become a . . . a . . .

"Go ahead, Kelly," Giambroni urged her, "Say the word. Vampire. Nothing will happen. Vampire, vampire. See? No lightning bolts filled the sky. No celestial sirens went off. Come on, Kelly, we need you. We need your sense of humor to remind us to enjoy ourselves a little. Being a vampire can be a weighty responsibility. Sometimes we take ourselves too seriously and we fail to enjoy . . . um, life."

No fear, no worry. Freezing squirrels. Zit-free skin. You people have to be kidding. This has to be a joke. That's when she noticed the angled shaft of light slicing through the window and falling across the long lab tables. Vampires can't stand daylight. Something's going on here, something really weird. I know, I've been set up for one of those TV shows. That has to be it. She looked around to find the video recorder. They want me to start acting goofy or scared or something.

"A myth," Giambroni said.

Kelly looked at him quizzically.

"All that nonsense about us hating light. It's a myth. A handy one, since you normal people never suspect us of anything. We live ordinary, dull lives like everybody else. And we don't change into bats at night or sleep in coffins or cringe in terror when we get too close to garlic. Imagine me not liking garlic." A huge laugh erupted from Giambroni and Marissa, Trish, and Jeannie joined him. "But some things are true. We do have certain powers" — he turned to stare at Trish — "although some of us have been neglecting our lessons."

"Mr. Giambroni, I've tried, really I have. But I've been having so much trouble with freezing the squirrel I don't have time for the other stuff." She bit her lip nervously. "And then I have cheerleading and piano lessons and my other school studies."

"That excuse might work with your algebra teacher, Trish, but not around here. You have to concentrate on what's important, understand? You'll have time later for those other interests." He came back to Kelly. "That's another thing. You'll have plenty of time to do anything you want. I could tell you stories about the good old days in Rome that would curl your hair. But that can wait, I suppose. Right now the important thing is for you to join us."

No, no, no, no, no. This is bad. Sucking blood is evil, killing is evil.

"Evil? No, I don't think so. As for killing, well, it happens now and then," Giambroni admitted. "Sometimes we take too much blood in all the excitement. But if you're careful that won't happen. The donor will feel a little weak, that's all. They won't even remember what happened. And they don't automatically become vampires either. That's another myth. Yes, you have to be bitten, but the most important thing is that you have to want to become a vampire, really want it, before it happens. What do you say?"

Kelly stared at him for a long time, her thoughts a jumble. It all sounded so inviting, so safe and simple. Still, a negative cloud swirled around inside her head. And if I refuse, Kelly asked, what then? One of those little mistakes?

"Oh, no, no. Not at all. A little nip and you'll forget everything. Even the cafeteria." He waited but she did not think of anything to say. "I can see we have to bring in the big guns," Giambroni said, snapping his fingers again. Almost instantly, a figure entered the room and moved toward Kelly. He was tall and handsome and had piercing blue eyes.

Brian! You, too? You're one of them?

"A vampire," he said casually. "Yep."

But why become one of them?

"Why not? There are no drawbacks. Just pluses."

What about the blood sucking? What about eating mice raw — she gagged slightly, remembering the tail twitching just before Giambroni swallowed him — how can you do that? It's revolting.

"It was hard at first," Brian admitted. Suddenly, he looked as helpless as he did in the cafeteria. "Once, early on, I killed this cat . . . my little sister's cat. It was an accident, honest, but I still felt bad, real bad. I couldn't sleep for days. But it got easier, especially when Mr. Giambroni pointed out how humans kill living things all the time. Think about it, Kelly. There was a time when your hamburger was standing in some quiet field, minding its own business and munching grass. And where do you think your shoes and belts come from? And the fur coats people wear? And how about lab animals being used for experiments? I could go on and on, you know. The bottom line is that we're all involved in cold-blooded murder in a lot of ways." Brian shrugged, then his expression brightened. "Anyway, Mr. Giambroni says I can be a professional football player someday."

"With practice," Giambroni pointed out.
"You will have extraordinary physical powers,
and they will need to be shaped very carefully.
But it will happen. In fact, you might very well
become one of the best quarterbacks in the
history of the game. Just look at what Joe Montana has done with his . . . um, special powers.
You could be even better than him."

"Better than Joe Montana," Brian repeated reverentially. He turned to Kelly.
"You've got to say yes, Kelly. You've got to.
It's great. Ask Marissa. Ask Trish or Jeannie."

"Brian's right," Marissa said. "I've never
been happier, never felt better. Remember how
I used to always get headaches when I was nervous. I haven't had a headache in weeks. And
I'm just beginning my vampire career."

Trish agreed, adding, "No late night cram-
ming for tests, no feeling left out of conversa-
tions either. Neat."

"And you'll have skin to die for," Jeannie
said and immediately started to giggle. "Well,
you know what I mean."

They sound like a TV commercial trying
to convince me their product is the best. Next
they'll offer a money back guarantee. She
looked past them and into Brian's eyes. They
were a startling color of blue, so deep, so intense, and charged with magnetic power. She
had wanted to get to know Brian, to go out with
him. And here it was being offered to her. I

wonder if he likes me, really likes me, Kelly thought.

"I do," Brian said. "I've wanted to talk with you since I came to Ben Franklin. Now we can be together."

For a *very* long time, Kelly thought.

"That's right," Giambroni reassured them. "But I don't want you kids getting too serious for a hundred years or so." His laugh filled the room again and Kelly felt herself relaxing. What's the big deal, she told herself. I had a harder time making the field hockey team.

"Will you become one of us?" Brian asked hopefully. "We'd like you to. I'd like you to."

Kelly felt her fingers begin to flex, then her legs began to feel stronger, more responsive to her commands. Her vocal cords loosened and felt normal. If she could duck past Brian, she could make it to the door and scream for help. Of course, then she would lose Brian forever. Besides, they seemed to need her.

"We're going to have a great time," Brian said. "A great time. Relax, give the idea a chance. Nothing bad will happen to you. Trust me."

I do, she thought. I do trust you. So just say yes, she told herself. The word didn't come out. My parents. What about my parents? I don't want to leave them. Not now anyway.

"No problem there, Kelly," Giambroni said. "We all lead our regular lives otherwise. We have families, we mow the lawn, we barbecue steaks. Rare, of course. You can stay with your family for as long as you want. That's the beauty of it all."

"And if they're ever angry with you," Trish said, "you just give them a nip and they'll forget everything."

"So what do you say, Kelly?" Brian asked. "Will you become one of us? Will you become a vampire?"

The answer took shape deep in her brain, swirling around with memories of what her life had been, what her life would become, the new things she would have to learn to do. There was still something dark and evil in all of this, yet it was no longer clear what that was. A teacher would never mislead her. Her best friend would never get her involved in something that would hurt her. And Brian . . . those blue eyes would never lie to her.

"Say yes, Kelly," Brian urged her. "Say you'll become one of us."

"Ah . . . I'm not . . ." The clouds of doubt suddenly broke and scattered, and her mind flooded with warm light. "Yes," she said, her voice so strong and firm it startled her. "I want to become one . . . become a vampire."

While Marissa, Jeannie, and Trish congratulated Kelly, Brian moved closer until he stood face to face with her. He was smiling at her, glad for her. He took hold of her arms gently, then his face came toward hers. Kelly prepared herself for his kiss, their first, but just before she closed her eyes she saw his mouth part slightly to reveal daggerlike fangs. Then a pin prick of pain shot through her neck.

The pain disappeared a second later and a strange energy began to infuse her body, creeping down her arms to her fingertips, filling her legs with a strength and power they'd never had before. She felt as if she could do anything. How could she have ever doubted her friends?

Brian leaned back, a tiny drop of blood at the corner of his lips. Her blood. Yet it did not startle her, or frighten her. She was one of them now.

Giambroni edged past Brian and put his hand on Kelly's shoulder. "Welcome to the club," he said, smiling. "You won't regret it one bit, Kelly. Not in a million years."

▲ 3 ▲
DIGGER IN PARADISE

So what did you think of the story? Oh, never mind, never mind. Forget I asked. I don't know about you, but I hate when people ask me questions like that since they don't really want to hear the answer. Not a real answer, that is. They want to hear a compliment, something nice and fuzzy, and I like nice and fuzzy about as much as I like a boil on the tip of my nose. Anyway, if you hated the story you probably wouldn't have bothered to read this far.

Where was I? Oh, yeah. I ran the Garrison Cemetery for a bunch of years, four or five if the gray matter is still working, and I was doing real good thanks to the yellow fever epidemic. You see, when the fever hit town during my second summer — that was in 1931 if you're adding and subtracting dates — nobody wanted to work in the cemetery. In fact, nobody even came to see their relatives buried. I guess they were afraid they'd catch something from the grave.

Town got mean, too. You see, nobody but the oldest people could remember anyone ever getting the fever, so when it started again, everybody wanted to blame someone. That someone turned out to be Jeremiah Ritter. Jeremiah had just gotten back from a yearlong trip to places like Burma, Borneo, and Thailand. At first, folks thought he was a hero for traveling the world. Even got his picture in the town paper. But when the fever started carrying off people, the town decided Jeremiah had brought it back from one of those hot, steamy places. People got so angry that they ran him out of Garrison, then burned his house to the ground.

Can't say that I blame them really. I was even a little worried myself. You hear stories about the fever victims — tongues swollen and turned brown, throwing up stale, black blood day and night until their stomachs rupture — and it makes you wonder. Even thought about quitting once or twice. Then the owner doubled my pay to keep me working.

I have to admit I liked the money. I was making about six times what my father was making at the mill, and it felt real good to be doing that and not even be old enough to vote. Truth was I liked the work, yellow fever corpses and all. All I had to do was make sure the holes were dug on time and keep the place looking neat. Pretty simple if you think about it.

So, of course, I stayed. That is, until things started to get bad. No, not at the cemetery. At home. I think my father was annoyed I was making so much more than him. He started making fun of my job, calling me names like "The Garrison Ghouly" and "Mr. Graves." Clever stuff like that. Then one day he goes and grabs my pay envelope right out of my hand and stomps out to get real drunk.

Now I had already been giving my mother more than half of my pay every week. It's only right that you pay your fair share if you live someplace. But *all* of my money didn't seem fair to me. Naturally, I said this to my father when he came home. He mumbled something about snot-nosed kids and took a swing at me. Fortunately, the blast that had gotten me my job promotion also taught me the value of ducking down quick, which I did. After missing, my father cursed me a few times and then wobbled off to bed. My mother was there, but she didn't do anything except shrug her shoulders and say, "You know how he gets at the end of the week."

That was the day I knew I had to leave. That was also the day I saw an ad in the newspaper for Prospect Hills Cemetery in a town called Guilderland. If you're interested, Guilderland is up near Albany, New York, and was this quiet, tiny village then. They needed someone to run the place and I figured that digging holes there was probably just like digging holes here. So I wrote the owner and three weeks later I was hired.

I have to admit I was a little nervous about leaving Garrison. After all, family is family, even if they take a swing at you for telling the truth. And working in the Garrison Cemetery felt good, like a really comfortable pair of work boots. But when I got to Prospect Hills I knew I'd done the right thing.

The entire cemetery was a series of grass-covered, gently rolling hills, and there were huge sycamore trees everywhere. All of the gravestones were tall and skinny, and made of the whitest white marble you've ever seen. It was beautiful, the white against the green. Best of all, I got to stay free of charge in a brick house smack in the middle of the gravestones. It wasn't much of a house really. More like a big tool shed with a room on top. But it had a porch in front that overlooked the oldest graves in the place, some going back to before the Revolutionary War.

I remember sitting out there during nights in October. As soon as the sun went down, the air turned real cold and fog started moving in. You could actually see it creeping around the gravestones, like long, filmy fingers, filling up the little valleys before climbing up the next hill. It was over there, over by a grave so old that the writing on the stone had faded to nearly nothing, that the next story took place. At least, that's what I was told. A hearse driver told it to me one day to pass time, but I never bothered to see if the story was true or not. It didn't matter to me. All I knew was that I had found Paradise.

▲ 4 ▲

GOOD NIGHT, JON;
SLEEP TIGHT, JON

Jon stood in the shadows next to the school, waiting. Where are they, he wondered, impatient and edgy. All nine of his friends, plus the newcomer, Troy, were supposed to be here at eight-thirty. He glanced at his watch.

"Jeez," he muttered. His mother had given him an expensive Swiss watch for his last birthday, one that somehow lit up all the numbers on the dial. It was experimental, she had explained proudly. Well, the experiment failed, Jon thought. For the past few hours, the numbers had been blinking on and off, like the pulse of some dying old man, and the only way to get it fixed was to send it all the way back to Switzerland.

Jon stepped away from the building to look up School House Road for signs of the guys. He'd chosen the meeting spot carefully — a dark dead end with few houses just a hundred yards from the rear entrance to the cemetery.

Once everyone was here, it wouldn't take but ten minutes or so to get to the cemetery and in place. It was the timing of the whole thing that worried him. His plan depended on precise timing. That's why Jon had had Deek trail the caretaker of the cemetery, an old guy known only by his first name, William.

According to Deek, William went on only one nightly tour of the grounds. He left his caretaker's house at exactly five minutes past nine — rain, sleet, or fog. Most important, he never varied his route; day after day, he took the same paths, stopped at the same graves. If Deek had this right — and he'd better, Jon thought, or he'll pay — then Jon had to maneuver everybody, especially Troy, into their positions at least five minutes before this. Better make it ten, Jon told himself. Deek had a habit of messing things up.

The fog had thickened into a dense, impenetrable soup, so his glance up School House revealed nothing. Even the bushes ten feet away looked like hulking, distorted shapes. What else can go wrong, he thought. He had wanted fog, but not this thick. If that old coot William can't see, he might walk right past Troy and then what? At that moment an icy drop of condensed fog splattered on his neck and slid down his back.

"Jeez," he shouted, dancing away from the building. He was about to release a string of frustrated curses when he heard a noise and froze. Footsteps. But they were coming from the cemetery.

Jon slithered behind a bush, arched his back, and held his arms straight at his sides. Probably some adult out for a walk, he told himself, so be careful. All he'd have to do is get caught on school property and he'd be laughed out of the gang. Then nothing would stop Troy.

He held his breath, listening for the footsteps, hoping he hadn't been spotted. Seconds dragged by but he didn't hear anything. Dead quiet. Probably waiting for me to make more noise, he cautioned himself. Go slowly. Don't be tricked. Carefully, he leaned around the bush and searched the fog. That was when the hand clamped onto his shoulder from behind.

"Oh, jeez, jeez," Jon screamed. He whirled around to face his attacker, but slipped instead and landed in a puddle.

"Hey, man, take it easy. It's just me," an adenoidal voice said.

"Who are you?" Jon demanded, jumping to his feet. Then he saw the glow of the cigarette and knew who it was.

"Deek, you jerk! What do you think you're doing?" Jon lunged at Deek, raising his fist to pound the glowing cigarette into Deek's face. "I'll kill you. . . ."

"Hey, Jon, hey, I'm sorry, man." Deek put his hands up to shield his face and continued pleading. "I didn't think I'd scare you or anything, honest."

Jon held back his punch and stood towering over the quivering Deek. He wanted to slam Deek into the ground, pulverize his face to prove he wasn't scared of anything, least of all a tap on the shoulder. But he didn't. He needed Deek right then. Let it go, he told himself. Save it for Troy. Save it all for Troy.

"What did you do that for, you idiot?" Jon mumbled. "And where have you been? And where are the others? And why were you coming from the cemetery?"

Deek peeked from behind his hands, then straightened when he was sure he wasn't going to be hit.

"It was Troy, Jon. He's the one."

"Troy?"

"Yeah, Troy. He said that to meet you here meant we had to walk all the way around the cemetery, and he said he wasn't going to waste his time doing that. That's what he said, Jon. Said if you wanted to have a meeting you could have it in the cemetery."

Jon felt that anger building again. He needed to hit something, or someone, but he also knew it wouldn't solve his real problem.

"And the others?" Jon asked. "Is everybody with him?"

"Yeah," Deek said. "We sorta met at Ian's and when we got to the cemetery Troy said what he said. I don't think everybody wanted to — I know I didn't, Jon — but you know how it is."

"Yeah," Jon said. "I know." Troy was winning them over, taking control, taking away Jon's power. Well, tonight he'd put a stop to it. He reached into the shadows and grabbed the shovel he had leaned against the wall. "Where's your shovel?"

"This is all I could sneak out of the garage," he answered, producing a garden trowel from his back pocket.

"Great. You're going to dig up a grave with a lousy trowel. Brilliant."

"My father was all over me tonight. Wanted to know where I was going, who . . ."

"Save it." Jon shook his head and left the shelter of the bushes. "C'mon, let's get moving."

"Sure, Jon, sure. Whatever you say."

For several minutes, the two walked down the street in complete silence. All the while, Jon was inhaling air and trying to calm himself. Time was running out. His time. He had to make this chance count. To do that, he had to be in complete control of himself and the situation. That reminded him of the caretaker's schedule, so Jon looked at his watch. It was still blinking away, broken and useless.

"What time is it?" Jon asked impatiently.

"Ah, it's . . ." Deek's watch didn't glow, so he had to hold it an inch away from his eyes. "Eight-forty, I think."

Jon let loose a string of curses and whacked the sidewalk hard with his shovel.

"There's still time," Deek said quietly.

"Hmmm." Jon and his friends had been hanging around together since elementary school. The Terrible Ten they had called themselves back then. They were too old for silly names now, but they were still a tight-knit unit, with Jon calling all the shots, mainly because he could outmuscle everyone. Then Troy appeared three weeks ago, a new kid in town. Immediately he began questioning Jon's decisions, making sarcastic remarks whenever Jon said or suggested anything. With each jab, Jon could feel his power over the others lessening.

Ordinarily, Jon would have squashed anyone who acted like this in a flash. But Troy was different. He was three inches taller than Jon and had the strength of a bodybuilder. A direct challenge would get Jon a mouth full of teeth and, worse, would leave no doubt that someone else was in charge. No, he'd have to outthink Troy, make him look like a fool, in order to regain control. The best part of it all was that Troy had suggested the idea himself without even knowing it.

Jon felt himself smile at the thought. For some reason or other, the name Asia Andrew Bingham came up while the guys were talking and Troy didn't seem to know who he was. It was a tired old story, but Chris told it as if it were today's headlines. In the old days, the story went, people were buried with their jewelry still on — gold rings, pearl necklaces, ruby brooches, whatever they loved to wear. Thousands and thousands of dollars in precious metals and gems had gone to the grave with dead owners, sealed in the fetid darkness for eternity. One night, a couple of locals decided to relieve the dead of the burden of their jewelry, and they began their treasure hunt by digging up the grave of a recently deceased man by the name of Asia Andrew Bingham.

Asia had been a wealthy dandy noted for his fine clothes, expensive boots, and imported hats. But his trademark about town was a carved gold walking cane topped with a glittering diamond. Asia never went anywhere without his cane and everyone, including the two grave robbers, assumed that meant his coffin, too.

Well, these two men dug into the soft earth and uncovered the wooden coffin in less than an hour. They used their shovels to pry off the top, then held their lanterns over to view their newfound fortune. It was there, of course, but so was Asia, his skin already an ugly yellow-blue, his nails long and clawlike — and his eyes wide open and glaring at the intruders.

No one really knew what happened after this. The men were never seen again, disappeared as if they'd been sucked into the earth. The only trace of them ever found was ragged bits of both men's clothes and blood smeared all over the empty coffin that had once been Asia's eternal resting place.

"They say," Chris had concluded his story, "that opening his grave released the spirit of Asia Andrew Bingham into the night and that he walks the cemetery to this day, guarding the graves from anyone who might try to rob them."

It wasn't anything Troy said after the story that alerted Jon to the other boy's weak spot. It was a look in Troy's eyes, almost as if he believed all of the hooey about spirits. He's scared, really scared, Jon realized, and instantly launched the challenge. Let's find his grave and dig it up to see if Asia's bones are there, Jon suggested.

Everybody had protested the idea, especially Troy. Grave robbing was a crime, a felony even. You could do serious time for playing around with bones. But then Jon had asked what everyone was afraid of, the evil spirit of the cane-wielding Asia Andrew Bingham? What's the matter? Are you chicken or what? This last had been said to the whole group, but Jon had been staring directly at Troy.

"You remember what you have to do?" Jon asked Deek as they entered the cemetery. "You'll have to move fast if you're going to get Troy into position."

"Sure, Jon. It's easy. You're going to head directly toward the caretaker's house, so Troy will probably hang back a little like he's not taking orders from you. Everybody else acts like they don't know where Asia what's-his-name . . ."

"Asia Andrew Bingham. You got that, Deek? It's important. It'll get his attention."

"Yeah, that's right. Everybody acts dumb so I can point it out to Troy. He'll want to be a big deal and be the one to dig it up and I'll help him a little, but mostly I'll act scared and say I hear noises and stuff. Right?"

"And?"

"And, oh yeah, so we do this a while, but I listen for the signal, that bird whistle you do, 'cause that means William is on the way and I have to beat it without letting on that anything's happening."

"Good," Jon said. He could see it clearly. Troy digging away, distracted and annoyed by Deek's whining, not knowing that the caretaker always made a special stop at Bingham's grave on his rounds. At the very least, Troy would have to make an undignified sprint to escape the old man. But if Jon was lucky, the caretaker would use his shotgun, putting a load of rock salt into the seat of the fleeing Troy. He'd never live that down.

They made their way around several gravestones. "Where are they anyway?" Jon asked.

"I left them over by the stone bench. The one with the angels carved on the arms and the . . ."

"Yeah, yeah, Deek. I know." The fog seemed even denser in the cemetery, especially in the valleys between the hills. The moisture made the grass slippery and Jon had to grab onto gravestones to keep from falling. They went over a few more hills before they heard voices and laughter in the distance. The next instant, the shapes of the guys materialized standing around the stone bench. While no facial features were very clear, Jon could tell that it was Troy sitting on the bench as if he were a king holding court. Once again, his anger flared.

"Keep it down, you guys," Jon barked when they got to the bench. "William might hear you."

There was sudden and absolute silence for a second. Then Troy said, "Relax, Jon. Nothing's going to bite you out here." Troy punctuated his remark with a chuckle, which some of the others imitated.

"I'm not kidding. That old fart isn't deaf and he really will use his shotgun."

"I don't think Jon is worried about any old human with a shotgun," Troy tossed in. "I think Jon is worried about the evil spirits that haunt the graveyard." Troy made a low, mournful, howling noise that ended in hysterical laughter. The other guys joined in, a little too easily and loudly as far as Jon was concerned.

Jon was so angry he could feel his veins pumping, and his breath came in short gasps.

If it was anybody else, anybody, he would have answered with a fist and then maybe taken on a couple of others just to set everybody straight. Save it, he told himself. Save it all.

"Look," Jon said, as calmly as possible, "we better make up a plan and get going."

"Plan? What's to plan?" Troy asked, getting up from the bench, his shovel clanking against the stone, and pushing past Jon. "We're going to find Asia Andrew Bingham's grave and take a peek at his bones. I say we stop wasting time and get going."

Jon stood, watching as Troy's body melted into the dark and fog. He's just acting brave in front of the guys, but that'll change when he comes face to face with William and his shotgun. A few of the others took a step or two to follow Troy, but then turned to see what Jon would do. Good, Jon thought. I still have a chance.

"Ian, why don't you take Chris, Eddy, and Brian and look over that way to the right."

Ian paused for a second or two, then said, "Yeah, sure, Jon. Sounds good to me." He hoisted his shovel over his shoulder. "Come on, guys."

"Scott and Elliot, check out the stones to the left. Mike, you and Jeremy, there are some really old graves behind us by the fence."

When everyone had disappeared, Jon turned to Deek. "You're going to have to move

fast, you hear? And make sure it sounds natural
or he'll suspect something."

"Don't worry, Jon," Deek said eagerly.
"I've been practicing what I'd say since you told
me and I even . . ."

"Stop yammering, Deek, and get going.
And don't screw up, you hear?"

"Ah, yeah, Jon. I hear you." Deek trotted
down the path Troy had just taken, his trowel
clutched in his right hand.

He's hopeless, Jon thought, but he does
what I say. Suddenly, Jon noticed how quiet the
cemetery had become. No breeze stirred the
leaves, no night birds called to each other. It
really was a little creepy being all alone, surrounded by gravestones that stood like senti-
nels on guard.

A noise to his right made Jon spin and he
was certain he saw something float through the
air and then vanish. It wasn't just a stray wisp
of fog. More ghostlike. Stop it, Jon cautioned
himself. Probably just a bat, and not the vampire kind either.

He turned and began moving up the path.
A feeling of satisfaction came over him then,
knowing that the plan was finally in motion. Not
far along he came to the large clump of laurel
bushes that concealed Asia's grave. As he
passed he heard voices.

"I can't see anything," Troy was grumbling. "You sure this is it?"

"Pretty sure," Deek replied. "I kind of felt

the old writing, see, and there were three names and one had a big A at the beginning."

"This better be it or I'll . . ."

Jon moved along. Dumb slab of muscle had fallen for it, just as Jon had expected. In a couple of minutes he'd shove Deek aside and start digging — and then it was William's turn to perform.

A little way up the path Jon caught a faint glimpse of lights in the distance. William's house. Next he came to the big sycamore whose roots snaked out across the path. This was it. Behind the tree the hill rose sharply. Jon could hide behind a gravestone at the top and still see William coming down the path. Once the signal was given, all he had to do was pivot his body around to watch the show Troy and William were going to put on.

He was halfway up the hill when his feet slid out from under him and he went down with a thud and a grunt. A string of curses filled his head as he struggled to pull himself up. That's when he saw it. Thirty feet to his left something scurried between the stones. There had even been a faint noise this time, the padding of feet on damp leaves.

His first thought was that it was William, taking a new route that would mess up the plan. But William never, ever changed his route according to Deek. Probably just some animal. A raccoon or stray dog. The cemetery was a regular zoo at night.

Jon pulled himself up the hill and found a good stone to kneel behind. Just in time, too. As Jon settled in, he heard a door bang shut and then heavy boots clomping down wooden stairs. Yes, Jon thought, yes. It's going to happen.

He could give the signal now so Deek would be sure to get away. But Deek had seemed so wired tonight that Jon really didn't trust his acting ability. Deek might panic and let Troy know that something was going on. No, he wouldn't signal until William was at the laurel bushes. Deek might take some rock salt, but he was expendable if it meant that there was no way for Troy to escape.

He heard the noise among the gravestones again, this time circling around behind him. That wasn't any animal either. The sound was too loud, too much like some clumsy kid trying to tiptoe and failing miserably. Maybe one of the guys had wandered onto the hill by mistake. Just then a flash of color in front caught his attention. What's going on, he wondered.

Jon craned his neck to see all around him. He couldn't be sure, but he felt as if the gravestones had come alive with tiny movements here and there, five or six at least. The movements were too organized, too deliberate. Jon didn't like the way it felt.

His first thought was to call out to see if it was the guys from the gang. But he couldn't do that without giving away his position to William. Instinctively, he pressed closer to the cold marble.

Seconds dragged along until Jon heard footsteps, this time coming from below him on the path. He peered around the side of the stone and saw William, shotgun nestled under his arm, ambling through the fog. Hurry up, Jon urged William. They're waiting for you.

But instead of hurrying up, William stopped suddenly and gazed all around. He had heard something, too. Jon was sure. Otherwise, why was he searching the shadows and fog so intensely. Jon edged behind the stone. If I don't move, don't make a sound, he'll move along.

Leaves rustled behind Jon again, and before he could look around, there was a hiss, then a loud, ear-vibrating concussion as an M-80 detonated. Jon fell against the gravestone and was struggling to regain his balance when a string of firecrackers landed at his feet, bouncing along the ground in a jittery dance as each exploded. Through all the noise, Jon heard a whispered command, "Move it, move it. Let's get out of here." Troy's voice.

"You!" William's harsh voice shouted at Jon from the path. "You up there! I see you! Stay right there or else!"

Another string of firecrackers landed, their peppery explosions illuminating Jon clearly. William was already charging up the hill in Jon's direction, his big boots digging into the soft earth and providing good traction. Jon had only caught a glimpse of William, but he noticed that the old man had shifted the shotgun and was holding it in two hands now, the finger of his right hand on the trigger. Jon tossed his shovel aside and began running.

"Stop, boy! Stop!" William continued to shout. His voice seemed nearer, though the fog distorted sounds, made them bounce and echo in an odd way, so Jon couldn't tell how close he was exactly. "You can't get away, you hear?"

Jon dodged around several gravestones, hitting one sharply with his hand, bumping another with a hip. White fog and white gravestones seemed to melt together, his body moving too fast for his eyes to adjust and pick out safe routes. He was about to slow up some when he heard keys clinking together not more than twenty feet behind him. William's keys.

He pumped his arms wildly. He'd been set up by Troy, and Jeremy and Ian and all the others were in on it. Even Deek. I'll get Deek for this, he promised himself. I'll get them all.

He came to a patch of thin fog on the other side of the hill and Jon flew down it smoothly, and up the next. The sheer abandon of his running, the wild speed, gave him confidence. No way an old man could keep up with him. A few more fast bursts like that and he'd escape.

As he came to the top, William's shotgun roared. Rock salt pinged and burst on the gravestones nearby. Jon ducked his head, but not low enough. A few pellets caught him in the back of the neck. He lurched forward, off-balance, his skin stinging painfully. I'll get every one of them. Every one.

"Stay there, boy," William shouted from the foot of the hill. Jon heard the snap of metal. "Darn kids," William muttered. "Should lock you all away."

A second blast was fired and this one caught him square in the legs, a thousand bee stings tearing into his flesh, making it burn. He felt his legs buckle, his body lurching forward out of control while his arms flailed. He was about to go down in a heap, when a strong hand grasped the arm of his jacket and pulled him upright.

"This way," a voice hissed.

Jon took a series of stumbling steps, still being supported by his savior. They went down the hill, then cut across the next at an angle, sidestepping gravestones easily.

"Deek?" Jon gasped. Darkness and fog made the shape pulling him along black, imprecise. He looked short, like Deek, and had the same skinny build, but something was wrong. A powerful odor, a mix of damp mold and dirt, stuck in Jon's nostrils. "That you, Deek?"

"Hurry," the voice repeated, sounding hollow and distant. The crushing grip on Jon's arm tightened and the figure picked up speed, forcing Jon to run.

"Who are you?" Jon asked. That was when

Jon noticed the cane. Jon tried to yank his arm
free, but the figure's grip became viselike. "Let
go!" Jon screamed. "Let me go!" Jon dug his
heels in, but the figure seemed to lift him off
the ground and haul him over the top of the
next hill.

Jon swung at the figure, but his fist only
grazed the shoulder and did no harm. "Let go
you son of a . . ."

Before he could complete his sentence,
the figure whipped Jon around to face him, released its hold on Jon's arm, and instantly —
with a movement so fast Jon didn't realize what
had happened — used that hand to grab Jon's
throat. The fingers felt sharp and brittle as they
squeezed and cut off his air supply. Then the
figure drew Jon's face toward it.

What's going on, Jon wondered, his head
spinning. He tried to see his attacker, but the
face was a blur. Then, as if the fog had suddenly
cleared, the features became more and more
distinct. In the time it took to gasp, Jon saw
more than he wanted — the matted clumps of
hair on the side of the head, the dripping strips
of rotted, discolored flesh, eyes cloudy white
and oozing, the jawbone exposed and barely
joined to the skull by tendon and muscle. He
was staring at a living skeleton. Asia Andrew
Bingham's.

Jon snapped his head back in horror and
screamed, "What do you want? Help! Let me
go! Help!" He struggled frantically to break

free, but it was no use. Asia Andrew Bingham's one hand held Jon firmly in place.

Asia pulled Jon's face to within an inch of his, an act that caused Jon to become mute. Asia held up his cane so that its head was close to Jon's left eye. Even in the fog, Jon could see the gleam of gold and the sparkle of a diamond. Then, in a voice laden with two hundred years of decay and putrefaction and loathing, Asia uttered the words, "Grave robber."

"But . . . but . . . I . . ." The words came out as a series of gasping, frightened croaks. "I was only trying . . ."

With an irritated snarl, Asia hurled Jon's body forward and Jon found himself plunging down a shallow pit and crashing into an open casket at the bottom. His entire body ached with pain, his head throbbed, and he was gasping for every ounce of breath he could suck into his lungs.

"But . . . but I was . . . only. . . ." Too late. Asia had already flipped the casket lid closed and leaped on top of it. A moment later, he began driving in nails along the edge of the pine lid, one after the other, each about three inches apart. Through the rough boards, Jon could hear Asia digging into his pockets for nails, could hear him breathe the words "grave robber" over and over again.

"Let me out," Jon screamed, pushing and kicking at the lid with all the strength he could find. "Help me. Help me. Deek, Ian, help! I'm in here. Help! Jeremy, Scott, help! Help me, you guys, help me. Asia's got me in here. Can't you hear me?"

The pounding of the nails continued unabated until Asia had done a complete circuit of the lid. "God, can't anyone hear me?" Jon managed to gasp between gulps of air. "Can't anybody stop him, please?" Inside, the coffin was black, the air warm and close. Particles of dirt sprinkled between the cracks and onto Jon's face when Asia tossed his hammer aside and stood up.

"See you got him," Jon heard a muffled ancient voice say. "William?" Jon screamed. "Is that you? Can you hear me? I'm in here. Get me out." Jon kicked and punched at the lid. "Can you hear me?"

"That him?" William asked.

"Grave robber," came Asia's reply.

"You can't do this to me. I'll . . . I'll . . ." A shovel full of dirt hit the top of the coffin, and Jon went quiet.

"You planned to rob Asia's grave, you were the leader of them," William said. "I keep this grave open for the likes of you, and now you have to pay the price."

"No, you don't understand . . ." Another shovelful of dirt hit the lid. "Stop it, stop it! Let me explain. We weren't going to rob any graves. . . ." Another and another load of dirt pounded into place. "Honest. You're making a mistake. Listen to me. . . ."

"Save it, son," William called down into the grave. "I ran your friends off long ago. No one is going to help you now. No one."

"But we weren't going to do anything." Tears had begun to sting Jon's eyes and his words came out as halting whispers. "Really. You've got to believe me. We were only . . ."

"Grave robber," Asia hissed, the words cold and leaden.

"Oh, Jon," William said. "That's your name, right? I heard one of those kids say it before they ran off."

"Yeah," Jon said, sniffling. "What of it?"

"I just wanted to say good night, Jon. And, uh, sleep tight, Jon." This was followed by two distinct laughs and the rhythmic sound of dirt filling up the grave, one shovelful at a time.

Jon screamed some more, but in a few minutes the sound of dirt hitting the coffin disappeared and Jon, exhausted, gave up calling for help. He took a few gulps of warm, moist air and realized they weren't satisfying his need for oxygen. His heart pounded and sweat trickled across his face. Got to do something, he thought, but his brain did not offer any suggestions at all. Instead, it kept saying, "more air, need more air, need it fast."

Don't think, Jon commanded. Do. Do something, anything. Push. That's it. He had to push, but with more force than he could generate while on his back. He could roll over and, hunched on his knees, use his arms and legs together. Worth a try. But when he tried to move, his shoulder jammed against the lid of the coffin and would go no farther. He fell onto his back and closed his eyes.

What did I do, he wondered. I don't deserve this. Maybe one of the guys will tell what happened and someone will see the fresh grave and. . . . Maybe. It's possible. But they probably wouldn't say a word until he was officially reported as missing, and that might not be until tomorrow. His already labored breathing and the fuzzy way his brain was putting thoughts together told him that tomorrow would be too late. All I wanted to do was embarrass Troy. Stay in control. Instead . . .

He opened his eyes and saw it. A glimmer of light, faint and distant, down near his waist, promising an escape route. Even the tiniest crack might provide a gulp of sweet, fresh air, enough to survive the night on, enough to hope on. Groggily, Jon craned his neck up as much as the coffin lid would allow to get a clearer view. He would have laughed at what he saw, except that he had no strength. There on his arm his watch glowed, the numbers on the dial flashing again and again and again, like the pulse of a dying old man.

PARADISE LOST

No, the caretaker in the story wasn't me, and I never saw old Asia's bones either, alive or dead. Talk about crypt breath! But I like what happened to that kid. Served him right, if you ask me. It's hard enough keeping a cemetery neat without a bunch of kids digging it up.

So, anyway, I worked in Prospect Hills Cemetery for a long time, so long that I can't even remember how many years it was. Then one day the pastor who ran the First Dutch Reformed Church — they were the ones who owned Prospect Hills — came to tell me the cemetery had been sold to some local businessmen. Seems membership in the church had fallen to about five or six, so they couldn't afford to keep either the church or the cemetery going. Don't worry, he said, the new owners promised that everything would go on as usual.

I don't know about you, but when anyone tells me not to worry, the first thing I do is worry. And I was right, too. They hadn't owned the place a week when they announced plans to build houses on all of the unused land. Ask me, dead residents are nicer than living ones. The dead never complain about taxes or noise or their neighbors. Hardly ever anyway.

Next thing I know I'm traveling south, down to Summit, New Jersey, where they were opening a new cemetery and needed someone to run it. This was my first trip outside of New York, so I felt like I was going to a foreign land.

Summit was okay, loaded with big old houses, massive trees, and winding streets. But the cemetery, that was something else. They'd gone and cut down every tree on the land, leveled all the hills, and put in a boring grid pattern of roads. Place was empty, of course, not a gravestone in sight, so it looked more like they were fixing to build a housing development than a graveyard. The worst was that they wanted me to use a backhoe to dig graves.

I remember my first day working — sitting on the backhoe, the engine rumbling and kicking out black, oily smelling smoke — and looking over the empty cemetery. Didn't feel right, not at all. So I jumped off the machine — left it running, I think — quit, and started looking again.

I was lucky about jobs back then. Either that or grave digging wasn't on the top of everybody's career list. A week later I had a job over in West Orange, another Jersey town, at a place called Holy Conception Cemetery. The second

I saw it I knew it was just right for me.

It had hills for a start, some nasty steep, too. And trees. Lots of them. Oh, they weren't well-cared-for, beautiful sycamores, like at Prospect Hills, but they were big and rangy, mostly red oaks and maples and a few lindens here and there. I wouldn't call the place pretty neither, not by a long shot. The grass was patchy, with hard-baked clay in between. And no one had bothered to collect leaves or twigs for years. Even the gravestones seemed tired and neglected, just dirty gray slabs. One whole section of gravestones was leaning at an odd angle, as if the wind had blown them all back on their heels.

But the place had some good points. There were no machines to bother with and I got to live in this eight-room house inside the cemetery. Only condition was that I share the place with the former caretaker, who had retired and was allowed to live there free of charge for as long as he wanted.

The day I was going to move in I knocked on the door of the house even though I already had a key. Guess I wanted to show the old man some respect. When the door opened I found myself staring at this old, old black man.

He was short and hunched over, leaning on a crutch because his right leg was missing. He had the whitest hair I'd ever seen, not much, but white, and the darkest, most leathery skin you can imagine. You could tell that he'd spent most of his life outdoors doing hard labor. I'd never seen a black man before, not up in the country where I came from, so I must've eyed him funny-like for a long time. That's when he poked me hard in the chest with a long, bony finger. "Don't fool yourself, son," he said by way of greeting. "You'll be dead and dust long before this old dog is gone."

Of course, I liked him right away.

He took me inside, showed me around, and then we settled in front of the fire. It was the middle of spring, but a cold wind had swept in, the last of winter, and it felt real good to lean in close to the flames. He told me his name was Alan A. Crinslow and I asked him what the A in the middle stood for.

"Allan," he replied. I must have looked confused because he added, "Allan with two Ls. My parents didn't have any learning, see, so they weren't sure how to spell it. Gave me both figuring that one must be right and I could figure it out on my own later." He smiled at that, then started to laugh. I laughed, too, though I wasn't sure whether he was putting me on or not and I never asked either.

He was a good storyteller, too. Better than Clement even, which is saying a lot. Told stories about anything you could think of — the ghost that pushed over the gravestones, the way the trees talked to each other at Halloween, the huge dog that prowled the cemetery whenever there was a full moon. You name it and Alan

Allan had a story. In case you couldn't figure it out, it was Alan Allan who told me the next story. Swore it was true, too. Said I could go to the library and look it up if I wanted. 'Course, he had this smile on his face the whole time, and when he finished telling it he laughed and laughed and laughed.

▲ 6 ▲

LIKE FATHER,
LIKE SON

Brian paused a second in front of the thick, metal door before punching in the fifteen-digit security number. He was the only kid in his school, probably in the world, who had a vaultlike entrance to his basement. Then again, he was probably the only kid who had an Egyptian tomb in his basement.

Even in the dim, predawn light, he could see the oversized poster his father had taped to the door a week before. It was of the Sphinx, the half-man, half-lion creature whose staring eyes guarded the entrance to the Great Pyramids. Underneath, his father had penned a single word in big, bold letters: WOOF. Brian recalled the scene that had followed this feeble attempt at humor. His mother had flipped out.

"I have to live with that . . . that thing in the basement," she had said when she saw the poster. "Now it's in the kitchen. What next,

Leonard? Opet festivals in the backyard? Embalming on the second floor?"

"It's just a joke," his father had explained. "And downstairs is important to my work."

His parents had gone on arguing about "downstairs" for a while, but he didn't listen. Not after hearing the same thing for ten years. Instead, he looked at the poster and sensed there was more to it than a bad joke.

Father never, ever joked about downstairs, Brian had thought when he saw the poster. No, the poster was a sign that he had almost finished his project. He wants everything in place when the photographs are taken, and that includes the tomb's guard. His father always made sure that his research was carefully documented for publication, but Brian knew his father well enough to suspect the poster meant more.

His father guarded the secret code numbers passionately, like some big shot Egyptian priest. No one, not even his mother, knew them. Still, his father never missed a chance to show how much smarter he thought he was than everyone else. The serious research article on his latest project would probably have one cute touch. He could imagine his father boasting, "Anyone who truly knows these ancient people would have guessed that the poster was literally the key to entering the tomb. Of course, not many people really see what is right in front of them." I do, Brian thought, and I'll prove it.

And when I get downstairs, I'll prove I know something about Egyptian rites, too.

He clicked on the flashlight and aimed the beam at the keyboard to the security alarm. One mistake would set off interior and exterior alarms and notify the police department of a break-in, so he hoped his logic proved correct.

"No," he said softly. "No doubts now." He couldn't start second-guessing himself at this point. That was something his father already did too well. His theory would be absolutely perfect, and that was that.

Three thousand years ago the Sphinx was known by a different name — Hor-em-akhet. His father had only mentioned this one time, months ago, and probably didn't even remember doing it. But Brian did. And after seeing the poster and thinking about the name, he hit on what he was sure was the answer. If you disregard the dashes and assign each letter a number according to its position in the alphabet, you have it. H is 8, O is 15, and so on. He pushed the numbers — 815185131118520 — and waited tensely.

Nothing happened for a few seconds and Brian felt himself take a deep breath and hold it. If he couldn't figure out the entrance code, maybe his other ideas were all wrong, too. Then a tiny red light on the panel blinked three times as the alarm network was neutralized, followed by the sharp, metallic click of the dead bolt sliding back. Success.

Brian yanked the door open, pausing momentarily to allow his pounding heart to settle down and to be sure his sleeping parents hadn't been awakened by the sound. Then he stepped onto the small landing at the top of the stairs and let the door close behind him. By the time Brian reached the bottom, the security system reactivated itself and the door bolted tight again. His father did not like to be disturbed when he worked in the tomb.

Brian knew the procedure that followed by heart. First, kill the flashlight and light the torch stuck in the wall. All electricity in the basement had been removed eight years before, on the same day the washer and dryer were hauled up into the kitchen over his mother's protests. "You have to see it by flame," his father once stated. "It's how the Egyptians saw it, with torches, flickering light. The figures seem to dance in this light." His father's normally booming voice would turn to a respectful whisper when he talked about the ceremony, as if he might disturb the spirits of the tomb.

Next, Brian took the high priest's simple black robe from the hook and slid it on. Black was a lucky color in ancient Egypt, the color of the fertile Nile soil, a symbol of rebirth. After the robe came the solar crown, a sign of power and eternal life.

He had never touched the large crown before, let alone worn it. "It's been appraised at over $325,000," his father had told him.

"Solid gold and in perfect condition. No one is allowed to touch it, you hear?" Except, of course, his father. When you are the head of the university's archaeology department and the one who found Pharaoh Mernepath's tomb, you are allowed certain privileges.

Brian's hands shook as he removed the crown from its resting place in the wall. The center of the crown was a gold helmet, studded with rubies. Coiled on top was a gold cobra, its hood flared open as if about to attack, its eyes glittering diamonds. Ram's horns flared from either side of the helmet at about ear level. Topping each horn was a gold solar disc, polished to reflect the sun. The ornate structure wobbled when Brian put it on his head, so he had to hold it in place with one hand. With the torch in his free hand, he began moving down the entrance corridor, stopping every so often to light another wall torch.

The corridor was four feet wide, the same width as in the real tomb, and it hugged the three outer walls of the basement. This wasn't the same length or layout as the original, but it was the best his father could devise in their suburban basement. The most spectacular part of the corridor was the carved relief hieroglyphics that covered the walls from floor to ceiling — hundreds of strange, magical looking animals, shapes, and symbols, all of them massed here to praise the primal sun god, Re, and welcome Pharoah Mernepath to eternity.

They really did seem to move in the flickering torchlight and Brian had to remind himself that they weren't real, just poured fiberglass reproductions. The university had had them made for an exhibit celebrating his father's discovery of the tomb, then lent them to him afterward. He could still see his mother's expression as each slab was carried in and attached to the wood-framed outline of the tomb, while his father attempted to justify the twenty-five thousand dollars in construction costs. "The university said it could only go so far in funding an at-home project. And authenticity is vital if I hope to recreate the ceremony. Vital." His father's voice boomed loudly when he was in the kitchen trying to get his way.

When the torchlight filled the first corner, Brian stopped abruptly, startled, and had to clutch the crown before it toppled to the concrete floor. It happened every time he came to the corner and saw the dusty mummy of a slave hunched there, legs tucked up in a fetal position, head bowed slightly forward in respect. It was in the building code, his father had explained, dead serious; every corner of the tomb — and there were sixteen of them if Brian remembered correctly — had to have the mummy of a slave. Naturally, they were all on loan from the university, as was everything else in the basement.

Brian steered clear of the mummy and moved along the corridor, one hand balancing the solar crown, the other holding the torch in front of him. The ritual directed that the priest, in this case Brian, stop every third step to read the hieroglyphics. He did this, though his father had only taught him what a few dozen symbols meant, so he spent a lot of time guessing at the meaning of what he was seeing.

At the second corner of the passageway, he almost broke out laughing. The austere image of the god Amun-Min was placed exactly where the old Maytag had been. "Oh, great god of hot and cold water," Brian mumbled to Amun-Min, "may you spin dry forever in happiness." At last, Brian came around the third corner where a relief image of Horus, winged god of kingship and good luck, waited above the door to the tomb's antechamber.

He was supposed to say a prayer to Horus, some long involved thing, to prove that his intentions were good and to remove any protective curses that might be in effect. Sort of like his father's security system, Brian thought. Since he hadn't been able to find any part of the prayer in his father's study, he looked directly at Horus and said, "I'm okay. Honest, you can trust me." He ducked so the crown wouldn't bump the door lintel and stepped into the antechamber.

It was a tiny room, only ten feet by ten feet, so the torch illuminated every corner. It had been almost a year since his father had last escorted him through the tomb, so Brian paused to take in the furnishings. To his right were the large funerary couch and the inlaid chests that held the things Pharaoh needed for everyday living, his gloves, rings, wooden bowls and cloth. Jars for different scented oils and unguents crowded the floor. Their contents had long ago evaporated, but Brian remembered sniffing one of the empty jars and being surprised to detect a distinct roselike odor, thousands of years old. Immediately to his right was a wall of shelves, each holding the mummified remains of Pharaoh's beloved pets, his hunting dogs, hawks, crocodiles, rabbits, cats, pigeons, and monkeys. What was an afterlife, his father had explained, without companionship? The floor in front of the shelves was a jumble of clay containers for food, wine, and water. And, of course, as per code, each corner had its required slave. Not my idea of a fun job, Brian thought as he entered the next room, the burial chamber.

This was the largest room, taking up half the area of the cellar, twenty feet wide and almost sixty feet long. To his left, on one of the short walls, was a tiny window, the only one not bricked up in the basement. The window faced east so that as dawn came, light was cast across the length of the room and onto Pharaoh's sarcophagus. In the real tomb, entrance chamber, antechamber, and burial chamber were in a straight line, one after the other; when the outside door was open, morning light hit the sarcophagus. This little window, heavily barred to avoid break-ins, was the best his father could do.

There were six wall torches in the chamber, but Brian didn't bother lighting them. The ceremony allowed for only two small lamps to be lit, one to burn precious oils, the other to burn spices. Besides, the light beginning to seep through the window told Brian he didn't have much time. He put the lit torch in an empty wall holder, then went to get the alabaster chest from the treasury room.

It was a tiny room, too, and crammed to overflowing with gold statues, large fans, chests of precious jewels, and carved ivory reliefs of Mernepath. It always made Brian feel claustrophobic. Normally, seeing all of this wealth heaped together here took Brian's breath away. Today, he hardly even noticed. Instead he concentrated on keeping the crown on his head while dragging the alabaster chest into the burial chamber.

He was almost ready. He lit the two lamps and added the required oils and spices. While these heated up, Brian switched on his father's battery-powered tape player. Evidently, batteries did not spoil the ceremony. Soon the rhythmic chanting of the high priest's assistants began, accompanied by the mournful wail of goat horns calling the gods forth, and the thudding of drums to drive out evil spirits. It was an eerie sound, haunting and beautiful, yet disturbingly primitive and violent at the same time.

As the purifying smoke began to fill the chamber, Brian smothered the torch flame and opened the top of the alabaster chest. Inside were four compartments, one each for Pharaoh's preserved liver, stomach, lungs, and intestines.

His father should have listened to him, he thought. Brian had tried to tell him the ceremony had to start at daybreak. After all, the ceremony was to call forth Re and when better to communicate with Re than in the morning when he first appears. No, his father didn't think the time mattered, saying he hadn't found any mention of it in the hieroglyphics. Brian's argument that the precise time for the ceremony was probably a secret held by the high priest was brushed off with a typical adult phrase: "Brian, you really don't understand what I'm trying to do here."

Yes, he did, and today he would prove it. He would more than prove it. He would astonish his father. Twenty-five years ago, his father had defied the traditional beliefs of archaeologists and located Mernepath's tomb miles from where everyone thought it might be. He had used logic and mathematics and a knowledge of the position of the sun to locate the mountain where the burial had taken place. According to his mother, his father had been happy for a number of years while the tomb and its many objects were being excavated, catalogued, and set up in the museum. But then he'd grown depressed. "Beautiful objects," he had said, "that have a sense of vanished but haunting forces clinging to them. I want to bring those forces alive."

He didn't mean he wanted to bring Mernepath's mummy alive, just the feeling of his spirit. His father wanted to create the greatest museum exhibit in the world, one where visitors would not just view the inanimate objects of a great civilization. They would enter the tomb, be part of the ceremony, and really feel what it was like to be alive three thousand years ago and in the presence of Mernepath and the legions of priests and gods who attended him. Ten years had gone into recreating the tomb, researching the ceremony and music, and perfecting his skill as the high priest. Ten years during which his father had grown more secretive and strange. "There is no privacy at the museum," he had explained as the reason for building the tomb at home and for having an eight-thousand dollar alarm system installed. "People steal ideas as well as objects." His father insisted he was close, very close to having the ceremony perfected and ready to show.

Why stop with bringing back just the feeling, Brian wondered. The ceremony was supposed to be about energy recharging, of giving life back to Pharaoh, so logic told him that if you had the correct instructions, the mummy would rise from its coffin.

He went to the open sarcophagus that held Pharaoh's coffin. He'd need two hands to get the lid off, so Brian leaned the solar crown against the base of the sarcophagus and grabbed the chain with both hands. The chain and winch system was another modern convenience. After all, the lid to the sarcophagus was made of gold and weighed almost eight hundred pounds. Brian pulled and the chain made an ungodly clatter and squeak as the lid slowly lifted to reveal the mummy inside. He didn't worry about the noise giving him away; the basement was not only soundproof, but sealed tight against the outside world. An outdoor air-conditioning unit chilled air to the frigid temperature of the tomb, triple filtered it to remove dust particles, then pumped it into the basement through tiny vents.

The lid cleared the top of the sarcophagus enough to reveal the coffin inside. The coffin lid was lighter, made of wood with Mernepath's likeness carved on it, so Brian was able to yank it up easily to reveal the mummy. After missing the importance of the time of day, Brian thought, what was in the coffin was his father's second big mistake.

It was a mummy all right, its hundreds of yards of dusty, decaying linen wrappings covering the frail remains of a human. But it wasn't Mernepath. The university had loaned his father item after item over the years, a collection that the insurance company valued at

$1,700,000. But when his father asked for Pharaoh's body, the university had said no. Instead, they let him take the mummy of the overseer of Mernepath's household.

Imagine, Brian mused. You work day and night for a guy and when he dies, you, along with all of his servants and slaves, are put to death and wrapped for eternity so you can keep his afterlife clean, too. No, thanks.

It was the overseer's lowly position that had attracted Brian's attention. Egyptian life was severely regulated according to class, with slaves at the bottom and Pharaoh at the top. The same held true for the gods. Everyone had a place; everyone had a job serving those above them. His father had decided to implore the god Osiris, ruler of the afterlife, as well as Re, to rekindle the spirit of the mummy. Why would such an important god as Osiris bother with resurrecting a lowly overseer? Brian had asked. His father's response had stung like a slap in the face: "Brian, I don't have time for your childish notions anymore."

"Get ready for a live mummy then," Brian mumbled.

The chanting seemed to have intensified and when Brian checked the tape player he saw that almost three and a half minutes had gone by. His part in the ceremony began in three minutes. He'd have to hurry.

First, he pushed the statue of Osiris to the side of the sarcophagus. Next, he went back to

the treasury room and dragged the battered
wooden statue of Shu into the burial chamber
and placed it in front of the sarcophagus. Of all
the gods who had images in the tomb, he
couldn't think of one lower in stature than Shu,
god of air and wind. Anyway, he had the least
impressive-looking statue, no gold or jewels or
precious metals on it at all. Just plain unpainted
wood.

Brian put the solar crown back on and
opened up the piece of paper containing his
words. He'd found the paper hidden under his
father's desk blotter, written in hieroglyphics.
Translating it had taken Brian three nights and
he was shocked at how short it was. Just ten
lines. But when he said them his father would
never call his ideas childish again.

There was a change in the rhythm of the
drum beat, hardly noticeable really, signaling
that the high priest's part would begin in one
minute. Brian scanned to make sure everything
was in place — corridor readings done, solar
crown on his head, plenty of smoke pouring
from the two lamps, the coffin open, Shu in
place. That was it, wasn't it? He'd done everything required. So why did it feel that something was wrong?

Then he saw why. No sunlight was coming
through the tiny window to strike the sarcophagus. Clouds had drifted in to block Re's ap-
pearance and without him the ceremony would
go nowhere. But what could Brian do?

Nothing, of course. Except start the ceremony and hope for the best.

The chanting, drumming, and horn blowing had all intensified and swelled in volume and fervor. Brian allowed himself to enter into the sounds of the ceremony fully, to feel its pulse and energy. Each god's *ka*, or divine spirit, was being summoned. One at a time they would arrive, with the lesser gods showing up first. Shu is here, Brian thought. He has mingled with the fragrant smoke, filling the air, my lungs. He is swirling around the mummy and its organs, waiting for Re before entering the dead body and bringing it back to life.

The thought frightened Brian a little, made him feel light-headed. Did he really want to bring this body alive? What was he going to do with it when that happened? How could they begin to communicate?

Brian would have shaken his head to force the bad thoughts from his brain, but he was afraid the solar crown would fall off. "Idiot," he muttered instead. "You've thought of all of this." The overseer was barely five feet tall and over three thousand years old. Not exactly a fearful physical specimen. Besides, Brian's plan was to run to get his father the second the mummy showed signs of life. Did he still want to bring him back alive? You bet. Just seeing the look on his father's face would be worth it all.

Suddenly, the chanting, drumming, and

horn blowing stopped and the room became quiet. It was Brian's turn. Everyone is waiting for you, he told himself. Your assistants, the gods, the mummy. He felt their collective *ka* pressing in on him, choking off the air, making him feel hot and sweaty and weak-legged. He gulped in oxygen to steady himself.

"Umm," he stammered, his tongue refusing to form words properly. Did his father experience this when he held his ceremonies? Brian licked his lips, swallowed hard, and looked at the Egyptian words printed on the paper. Okay, here goes again. "User-Maat-Re," he said, mentally translating the words as he read them. "Strong in truth is Re . . ." Only where is he, Brian wondered, before plunging on with the rest of the prayer.

". . . Powerful is his spirit. Kind is his manner. We implore you, god of the eternal sun, enter this room to fill it with your power. Mingle with the *ka* of Shu, here before you. Possess the remains of your faithful one, Pharaoh . . . um, Pharaoh Mernepath's faithful overseer. . . ."

It was at this point in the prayer, as if staged for a cheap adventure movie, that the clouds outside broke up and the room began to brighten. Then a spectacular burst of sunlight filled the burial chamber, bouncing off the objects and sending shafts of dazzling brilliance in every direction. Brian glanced to his right and saw the treasury room glowing in the reflected light. Most important, the sarcophagus was bathed in sunshine, its hard granite surface radiant.

He located his place in the prayer. ". . . ah . . . faithful overseer, um . . . okay, okay . . . May his spirit be called forth from the afterlife. May his body be renewed through your power. May he shed the foul stench of death and be guided back to the living. Only through you, all powerful Re, can this be accomplished." Brian bowed his head as the instructions directed and repeated the opening line three times: "User-Maat-Re, User-Maat-Re, User-Maat-Re."

Head still bowed, Brian waited and listened. Not a sound. No stirring came from the coffin, no sigh escaped the body as it drew in fresh air. The burial chamber was as still and silent as it had been for the three thousand years before his father had found it. Dead air, dead body — and nothing more.

He'd failed. Miserably. His father was right; he really was just a kid who didn't know what he was talking about. His emotions began to sag, the positive energy that had brought him to this moment leaking away like helium from an old balloon. Then, unexpectedly, Brian felt his legs wobble and his body lurch back a step; the solar crown slipped from his fingers and crashed to the cement floor.

For a heartbeat, Brian didn't move. Then he was on his knees, fumbling to retrieve the crown and saying an altogether different sort of prayer. But it was no use. The crown had broken — the ram's horns shattered into thousands of little pieces, the solar discs breaking off and rolling along the floor, the cobra a twisted bit of metal.

He picked up a couple of pieces that belonged to one of the horns and fumbled to see if they fit together. How could he possibly explain this to his father? Well, you see, Dad, I didn't think you were right about the ceremony despite all your years of study and research. . . . He could already see the disgusted look his father would give him, see it turn to rage and hate, and he could hear the booming tones in which he'd scream at Brian for being so stupid, so childish, so arrogant, so . . .

There was a noise. Brian was certain he'd heard it. A rustling noise. When he raised his head, he heard it more clearly. As if someone was scratching to get out. It was too much to believe, too much to ask for. If the mummy was alive no one would be upset at what he'd done. Even the smashed crown would be overlooked.

Brian pushed himself up, only to discover that his legs would not yet support him. It's the smoke, he realized. The smoke from the lamps is doing this. He was able to press his face against the cold granite of the sarcophagus and reach his fingers to the top. He had to pull himself up, he had to see the mummy stirring to life so he could describe it. A grand and boundless joy filled him, made his heart pound uncontrollably. This must be what it's like to make a great discovery like his father had.

Slowly, he hauled himself up until his nose was even with the top and he was almost able to peer inside. The noise was louder now, more intense, a regular thrashing of arms and legs struggling to free themselves from thousands of years of restraint. Were those grunts and groans he was hearing, too? This was too good to be true. He leaned forward to see what the mummy was doing, then froze in astonishment. The mummy had not moved at all, not an inch. It was laying there, perfectly wrapped and as still as a carp.

But I heard it, Brian thought. Or have I gone completely crazy? He heard the noise again and realized he'd been tricked by the strange way noise bounced off the walls and traveled in the tomb. The commotion was coming from behind him, from the antechamber.

Brian turned just in time to see one of the mummified hunting dogs leap and catch a fleeing rabbit in its jaws as it tried to escape into the burial chamber. The dog yanked back and the rabbit's head snapped off, dust flying from the wrappings of victim and victor alike.

"What have I released?" Brian muttered. His angle of vision wasn't very good, but he could still see portions of the shelves in the antechamber. All of the animals had come alive and were rolling around, pawing and clawing and hacking at their wrappings. Some thrashed so much that they fell from the shelves and thudded to the floor where they continued their angry struggles for freedom. A crocodile slithered into the burial chamber, hissing and snapping its jaws. Logic had prevailed after all. Shu, the lowest ranking god in the tomb, had brought to life the lowest ranking creatures.

A cat entered the burial chamber dragging yards of linen. It saw the dog crunching away at the rabbit and joined him. Another cat sprinted into the chamber, wheeled around, hissing and clawing at the advancing crocodile. Several monkeys leaped over the fighting animals, their eyes on the shredded rabbit. Each trailed ribbons of linen, their exposed faces emaciated and drawn tight to reveal the bone structure.

And then, as if a silent command had been issued, all of the animals stopped what they were doing and turned their gaze on Brian. Scores of ancient eyes stared at him, then the animals began moving in his direction. I've done it, Brian thought. Not even Father could have freed them. I wonder if he'll like what I've done.

A hawk screeched and came soaring directly at Brian's face, his talons ready to rip into fresh meat. Appetites thousands of years old were about to be satisfied.

▲ 7 ▲

THE WORST DAY
OF MY LIFE

Working at Holy Conception Cemetery wasn't bad at all, though sometimes things got hectic. Like the winter we had three big snowfalls, real blizzards. People started freezing up right and left and I had to get a lot of holes dug in a hurry. Times like that, Alan Allan would help me.

Hard to believe, right? A one-legged old man digging graves in freezing weather. But there he was, jacket off, sleeves rolled up, and swinging a pick like a twenty-five-year-old in the middle of summer. 'Course, I laughed myself silly the first time I saw him in action. Wham! that pick would hit the hard earth and Alan Allan would start bouncing all around on his one leg trying to stay balanced. Wham! bounce, bounce, bounce. Wham! bounce, bounce, bounce. I almost hurt myself, it was so funny.

Alan Allan didn't think it was funny, so

he fixed me a stare that would have stopped a sixty-car freight train. "Keep on laughing," he warned, "and the next thing this pick hits'll be that head of yours."

Alan Allan had that look on his face when he said this, you know, the one halfway between being dead serious and pulling your leg. Since he had wiry strong arms for someone his age, and he could bounce along real fast, too, I thought better of pushing him too far. After that, I had to bite the inside of my cheeks to stop from laughing, and sometimes I had to make like I was having a coughing fit to hide the smile on my face.

Then it happened, like it always seems to. Like that saying goes, to every good thing there's something or other, I don't know, something not good, I guess. You can tell I'm not fond of wise old sayings. So one day I'm working along, happy as anything; the next day, the cemetery is completely filled. Not an inch of burying space left. Oh, I'd seen it coming for a couple of years. You couldn't miss it, the way the graves were eating up the space. No matter, it was still a shock when I dug that last hole and the owners said they'd be closing shop.

They offered to keep me on, said they needed somebody to pick up trash, rake leaves, and chase kids away. But I wouldn't feel right unless I was digging. Something about standing six feet in a hole that will be somebody's home for all time that made me feel good. Like I was making something that would last for eternity.

Anyway, before we begin a new hole we have to enter its number in a log book. This grave was number 4192, which also happened to be the exact same number of days I'd worked at Holy Conception Cemetery and the exact number of hits that baseball player, the one who went to jail for cheating on his taxes . . . what's his name? . . . oh, yeah, Pete Rose, got in his career. I'm not the superstitious kind, mind you, but this all struck me as too much of a coincidence, as if somebody somewhere was trying to tell me something. So the day number 4192 was done, I quit, pure and simple.

Wasn't easy leaving, but I figured the faster I did it the better. I packed my bag and headed out the door that same day, Alan Allan bouncing along behind me.

"What's your hurry?" he asked, but I think he knew and I think he agreed, too. Just before I was about to walk down the path and out of the place, Alan Allan shoves this fat envelope into my hand. "I thought you'd run out like this, so I wrote this story a couple of days ago. Only you can't read it now or anytime soon either. You can only open it when you're miserable, when you know you're having the worst day of your life."

"What if I never have a worst day of my life?" I asked.

"Then you can't ever open it, hear? Ever." I must have smiled or something because he added in this threatening tone, " 'Cause if you do, you will be cursed for all time by dark, dangerous forces. Now get moving, but don't forget what I said. Dark and dangerous forces."

Like always, Alan Allan smiled at the end, so I wasn't sure if he was joking or not.

"This isn't one of those shaggy dog stories, is it?" I asked. From my first day with Alan Allan, he'd been telling me weird tales about a wild dog that hung around Holy Conception, how it appeared only at night, and was trying to communicate with him. See what I mean about being weird? And lately, his stories were even stranger — something about eyes glowing red in the dark, and such.

"Wolf," he said, dead serious. "I told you it's a wolf."

"Sure," I said as I went down the stairs. "I've heard that New Jersey has a big wolf problem."

"Just wait," he called after me, "and you'll see." This time he didn't laugh or smile at all.

To be safe, I stuck the envelope in my back pants pocket and forgot all about it.

I'd always been lucky finding work before, but not this time. The war — this was the Second World War, in case you're counting — was just over, so there were lots of able-bodied young men floating around and some of them even went into the grave digging trade. A couple of places down in Maryland offered me jobs, but they wanted me to use machines to dig the graves. Seems the insurance companies decided it was too dangerous to climb into the grave and shovel out dirt like people had done for thousands of years. Now you had to use these big metal monsters that could cut your legs off if you sneezed at the wrong time. You figure it out.

I kept moving south, reading the newspaper ads and stopping in at every cemetery along the way. No luck. It was summer on top of it all, hot and humid and sticky with green flies smacking into my face from all sides. I was in South Carolina in a tiny town near the Coosawhatchie River when I just about gave up on grave digging.

You heard right. Almost gave it all up. There was a brand new textile plant just opened and a big sign out front said: NOW HIRING. I went in to see what jobs they had and before the man in the personnel office had time to see if I had a pulse he told me I was hired. Just like that.

Next thing I knew he was showing me where I'd be working — weaving machine no. 347. It was in this gigantic room filled with hundreds of other weaving machines, all of them clicking and clacking and thrumming along like one huge metal heart. The noise was deafening, and the personnel man suggested I stuff cotton in my ears during my shift if the noise bothered me. I knew I could never work in a place like that.

Don't get me wrong. Some good people
work in big factories and that's okay with me.
It just wasn't for me. Made me feel closed in,
trapped. Besides, I couldn't see going around
all day looking like a bunny rabbit with cotton
in my ears. I said thanks but no thanks and went
and sat on the banks of the Coosawhatchie,
watching the muddy brown water flowing by
and swatting at flies.

That's when I figured I was probably having the worst day of my life and it was safe to
open Alan Allan's letter. I read the first line and
you could have pushed me over and into the
river easy. Alan Allan wrote: "You're in South
Carolina right now, feeling worthless and trying
to keep the flies off."

How'd he know I was in South Carolina?
I wondered. Or about the flies? I mean, Alan
Allan is a smart man, but this was something
else. Scary even. I didn't want to read the letter
after this, so I dropped it on the grass and put
a rock on top of it. What if he predicted a tractor
pulling a plow was going to run over me and
shred my body into a thousand tiny pieces. I
figured if I didn't read it, it couldn't come true.

There I sat, the Coosawhatchie rolling
past, the flies buzzing around my head, the letter by my side. Minutes crept by and nothing
changed.

You could leave the letter here, walk
down the road to that diner and have some
lunch, I told myself, or you can sit here like a

lump and give in to your curiosity. What's it going to be?

Thinking takes time. At least it does for me. So I didn't move for another five, ten minutes. Somewhere in there I started to think other thoughts — stuff like, since this is the worst day of my life, then what Alan Allan has to say might put an end to it one way or the other. Besides, there was always something about Alan Allan's nasty little stories — even those dog stories — that cheered me up.

Slowly, I picked up the letter. My hand shook a little and I was nervous when I started to read. Alan Allan went on: "If this really is the worst day of your life — and it better be or else dark and dangerous forces will come for you — I figure you need something to cheer you up. So I wrote down this story just as it was told to me. I swear on the grave of the man who told me. He had a name for his story, but I forget it just now. If you want you can give it a name yourself."

So I did.

▲ 8 ▲

THE CAT'S-EYE

"This is boring," Kirsten said. She pushed herself out of the stiff chair she was sitting on and began walking across the living room toward the front door.

"You're not going, are you?" Jessica asked. "We've only been here a little while."

Kirsten stopped and turned to face Jessica. "You said we'd have fun, but all we've done is sit and watch these dopey cats sleep." Kirsten folded her arms across her chest.

"How was I supposed to know they'd sleep all the time?" Jessica glanced around and found the six cats still stretched out on the sofa, window sill, and rug, eyes closed and in no hurry to do anything interesting for their human company. "Mrs. Hayword said they can be a handful. Wild even."

"Wild!" Kirsten sighed dramatically. "I've had stuffed animals that were livelier."

Kirsten's voice caused Maurice, lounging on the thick oriental carpet ten feet from her, to open one green eye and stare at the source of annoyance. His eye never blinked.

"What are *you* looking at?" Kirsten asked. She took a giant step toward Maurice and stamped her foot on the floor. In a flash, Maurice snapped into a sitting position, both eyes wide open. Kirsten laughed at the cat's worried expression.

"Please don't do that," Jessica said. "Mrs. Hayword . . ."

"Mrs. Hayword, Mrs. Hayword, Mrs. Hayword. Can't you change the tune once in a while? You're about as much fun as the cats." She took another step toward Maurice, which caused him to sprint from the room. A look of pleasure lit up Kirsten's face, but only for a second or two. When it faded, she plopped back down into the chair. "Now what?"

Jessica searched the room, hoping she could think of something exciting to do. And fast. Ordinarily, Kirsten was great to hang around with — easygoing, loaded with energy, fast thinking, and daring. Oh, Kirsten could be a little bossy, but that was okay with Jessica. There was something about her personality, its power really, that made Jessica feel important. But you could never tell what Kirsten would do when she got into one of her impatient moods.

"Maybe there's something in the refrigerator," Jessica suggested.

"Worth a try," Kirsten replied, vaulting from the chair again. "Let's go see."

Jessica found herself following Kirsten out of the living room, through the dining room, and into a hallway that led to the kitchen. Mrs. Hayword's house was ancient, over two hundred years old, and big, with rooms and hallways being added for each new generation of Haywords who lived there. Jessica thought the house was neat, even the way the rooms tilted and met each other at odd angles and heights.

"What a dump," Kirsten said as she stepped down into the kitchen. The wooden floor was scratched and stained by the tread of hundreds of Haywords. "Forget cat-sitting. She should have hired us to redecorate."

Us? Jessica thought. Mrs. Hayword had really only hired Jessica for the job. It was Jessica who had persuaded the old woman to let her bring along her friend and split the five dollars an hour she was to be paid.

"I guess it would be all right," Mrs. Hayword had said, "as long as she's trustworthy. My cats and this house mean a great deal to me. They're all I have, really."

"Oh, yes, she is," Jessica had replied, hoping for the best. Now Kirsten was positioned in front of the old White-Westinghouse refrigerator, eyeing it suspiciously.

"Who has a refrigerator with a coil on top of it?" she wanted to know as she pulled the door open.

"She's poor. . . ."

"Oh, gross," Kirsten gasped, moving aside so Jessica could see what she was talking about. The lower shelf contained a few standard items — six eggs in a little green bowl, a half-loaf of white bread in its plastic bag, butter and cheese on plates sealed in Saran Wrap. It was the large middle shelf that had caused Kirsten's outburst. On it were six opened and partly used cans of cat food, each carefully labeled with a cat's name, each exuding an overpowering odor. Maurice's name was on a can of Yummums Chicken Livers and Kidneys.

"I think I'm going to barf," Kirsten said, making an exaggerated gagging sound. Before she could complete her performance, all six cats had assembled at the foot of the door and were meowing hungrily. Maurice edged ahead of the others and rubbed against Kirsten's leg. "Beat it," Kirsten mumbled, shoving Maurice aside with her leg and slamming the refrigerator shut.

"Kirsten!"

"I know, I know. Kicking the cats is strictly forbidden. Well, the least she could have done was have a can of Coke." Kirsten frowned and then started back to the living room.

It had been such a good idea, Jessica thought. She and Kirsten would make some money without really having to do too much work. She'd also get to spend several hours alone with Kirsten, which would give Kirsten a chance to get to know her. Really know her. Now Jessica was just one of twenty other fresh-

man girls who hung around with Kirsten. If
Jessica was lucky, she would go from just knowing Kirsten to being one of her best friends —
and that would be a major step up socially for
Jessica.

Kirsten stopped at a sideboard to open a
drawer and inspect the contents, and then again
at an end table in the living room.

Kirsten always was a little rude to people,
Jessica remembered, but it always seemed neat
before, especially when she did it to an adult.
She was letting everyone know she was in
charge, no questions asked. But this was different. She wasn't trying even a little bit to be
friendly to Jessica, and she was being paid for
it, too.

"Hey, way cool," Kirsten said as she held
something up to the light.

Jessica saw it glitter and moved closer to
get a better look. At least Kirsten had stopped
grumbling. "What is it?" Jessica asked.

"A marble. A cat's-eye. See?" Kirsten held
the marble up so Jessica could see but not touch
it. It was a clear crystal marble with a green oval
band in the center. Jessica had seen cat's-eyes
before but never one like this. The crystal part
gleamed so brilliantly it reminded her of a diamond, and the green oval wasn't just a flat
green. It really did look like an eye, with the
outside part, what would be the iris, a dark
forest green color, fading to a lighter shade of
green entirely, richer somehow and eternally

deep. If you looked at it long enough you felt as if you could fall right into it.

"Now we're getting someplace." Kirsten tossed the marble so high into the air its shadow danced across the ceiling for a second before it reached the top of its arc and headed back down.

"Don't!" Jessica shouted, lurching foward to save the crystal before it shattered on the floor. Only she never caught it. Instead, Kirsten stepped in front of Jessica and made a one-handed catch of the marble.

"Relax," Kirsten said.

Relax! Jessica thought, the anxiety of the past few minutes finally reaching the boiling point. "You . . . you . . ." she sputtered.

"All my friends know how to relax, Jessie," Kirsten added, smiling. "My really good friends, that is."

Really good friends? How could that be? Kirsten hadn't been having a very good time and now, all of a sudden, she, Jessica Elizabeth Wyman, was one of Kirsten's good friends. Jessica's mind raced, still annoyed with Kirsten and yet startled and joyous at the same time. She had said good, Jessica reminded herself. Not just friend, but *good* friend. And she'd called her Jessie, too. Somehow Jessica had done it. She'd entered the inner circle.

"You're a good sport, Jessie," Kirsten said. "Come on, let's explore this place." With that, Kirsten marched off toward the hall stairway.

As she did, she slipped the cat's-eye into her pocket and gave it a gentle pat.

"Kirsten . . ." Jessica began, then stopped. A good sport wouldn't badger Kirsten about taking a dumb marble. Jessica glanced at the open drawer of the end table and saw it was a jumble of papers, envelopes, rubber bands, coupons, string, and sewing needles. Maybe Mrs. Hayword wouldn't even miss it.

"Yeah?" Kirsten had stopped halfway up the stairs.

"Ah . . . wait up, will you?" Jessica slammed the drawer closed and hurried to Kirsten. "This place gives me the creeps."

"Tell me about it."

The second floor hallway was narrow, no more than four feet wide, and very long, with all ten doors on the floor closed. Kirsten and Jessica split up to save time and began racing into rooms, searching for the interesting, odd, or bizarre. Aside from an ancient white-tiled bathroom that had a toilet with an overhead flush tank, the rooms were all pretty ordinary. Every one had a small bed, a chair, an empty chest of drawers with a mirror, an empty closet and enough dust to say it hadn't been used in years. Only the last room in the hall was different.

"Everything's dust free," Jessica said after examining the furniture close up. "And the sheets look clean."

"Pay dirt," Kirsten announced, a smile

once again appearing. "This must be the old lady's room. She's got to have something worth finding in here."

She immediately started rifling through the dresser drawers, haphazardly pushing the carefully folded clothes aside. Jessica plopped herself down on the bed, content to watch. She'd given up trying to keep her new good friend in line, and she'd gone into several rooms she probably shouldn't have, but that didn't mean she had to ransack the place. One at a time, the cats entered the room and joined Jessica on the bed.

"I can't believe it. Nothing!" Kirsten announced after her first sweep of the room. She went back and did another search.

"Maybe we should go downstairs," Jessica offered, stroking Maurice's nape and getting a contented purr in return. "Mrs. Hayword said she'd be back as soon as she finished her business."

"It's locked," Kirsten said. She was at the closet, tugging at the door knob. "Why would she do that — unless there was something worth locking inside? Jessie, this is it! This is Old Lady Hayword's vault."

"She said it wouldn't take long. Her business. Maybe we should leave the closet till the next time."

"There might not be a next time." Kirsten was already kneeling and squinting into the key hole. "It's probably loaded with jewels and gold necklaces and stuff."

"Or bodies," Jessica added with a shiver.

"Bodies! Hey, neat. We'd be heroes, Jessie. All the papers would print our names. Imagine: 'Kirsten Richards, of Mount Holly Drive, Discovers . . .' "

"And Jessica Elizabeth Wyman."

"Sure, sure. 'Kirsten Richards *and* Jessica Elizabeth Wyman Discover the Rotting Corpses of . . . of . . .' " She looked toward Jessica.

" '. . . Of Every One of Their Teachers, Especially Mrs. Prune Face Eastman.' "

" 'Rotting, Smelly Corpses,' " Kirsten added, laughing. "So if you want to share the headlines with me, see if you can find the key."

"Well . . ." Jessica still wasn't sure about going through Mrs. Hayword's closet, but at least Kirsten had stopped complaining. And the closet couldn't be all that big judging from the others they'd looked into. They'd be in and out in a few seconds. Reluctantly, she went over to the chest of drawers and began looking among the brushes, combs, pin boxes, and bottles on the top.

"Try the drawers," Kirsten suggested. "I don't remember seeing any keys, but it might be worth a shot."

Jessica pulled a drawer open and began rummaging through the articles of clothes, already mussed up from Kirsten's initial search. "No keys in this one," Jessica announced before going on to the next drawer. Just then a tiny felt pin box fell to the floor, scattering its contents all over the place. When Jessica glanced up, Maurice was standing on top of the drawers looking smugly down at her.

"What are you doing, Maurice?" Jessica shouted. "Get off of there before you knock something else over."

"We should have done something with that flea catcher downstairs," Kirsten remarked.

"Kirsten, look." Jessica was holding a small, intricately designed skeleton key. "It was in that box, the one Maurice knocked over. Do you think? . . ."

But Kristen had already grabbed the key and was back at the door fitting it into the key hole. "Yes," she shouted. "It fits." The door swung open to reveal a tightly packed rack of clothes. "Well, at least he was good for something. Now to see if there's anything in here."

There was no overhead storage shelf, so Kirsten began going through the various boxes on the floor. Jessica came over and leaned against the door. "Anything there?" she asked.

"Shoes," Kirsten replied. She began patting down the clothes hanging in the closet, just like a policeman might do to a criminal. "Doesn't she believe in rings or watches or something? There isn't even a quarter in any of these pockets."

"She really is poor," Jessica said. "The house is all she owns."

"That's what they all say." She emerged from the closet and was about to slam the door shut when Maurice leaped between the two girls and disappeared inside the closet.

"Maurice, come out." Jessica was leaning over to see under the dresses and coats. "Come on, boy."

"Let's just close the door and leave him," Kirsten suggested.

"We can't do that. He might suffocate."

"Serve him right. . . ."

"Mrs. Hayword would notice he's missing right away."

"So what?"

"So she probably wouldn't pay us anything until she finds him, and then she'd know we'd been in her closet and . . ."

"Okay, okay, I get the picture." Kirsten pushed aside the clothes and called for Maurice. Then she saw that there was another layer of clothes behind the first. "This closet is deeper than it looks." She pushed the second layer aside to reveal another. When she stepped forward, the first row of clothes swung back to conceal her from Jessica.

"Kirsten?" Jessica leaned into the closet and moved the first layer of clothes aside. "Kirsten? Can you hear me?"

The second layer of clothes flew open to reveal a face just inches from hers and Jessica jumped back.

"You okay?" Kirsten asked. "You've got to see this, Jessie. It keeps going back and back, and it's loaded with stuff. She must have kept every dress she ever wore." Kirsten grabbed Jessica's hand and pulled her deeper into the closet. "There's a path between the clothes so we can probably get to the back of the closet fast. Then we can search every inch as we work our way out again."

"I don't know. . . ." But it was too late. Kirsten had gone ahead and for some reason beyond logic Jessica followed.

Kirsten was right. A foot-wide space between the clothes zigzagged along and made walking easier. The door to the closet was open, so diffuse light seeped in and let Jessica locate the path with little trouble for a while. Eventually, the light dimmed and an eerie dusk settled around Jessica. The temperature had also gone up and she felt sweat on her neck and forehead.

"Kirsten? Where are you?" Jessica stopped and began pushing dresses aside to see what was near her. A musky, stale smell surrounded her and she felt the dead air of the closet begin to make her breathing labored. "Kirsten?"

Jessica felt with her hand until she found a part in the line of clothes. She stepped into it, her hand groping in front for the path's route. Maybe Kirsten's lost in this mess, Jessica thought. She could turn around and find her way out, but what would Kirsten think of her then? Good friends don't abandon each other because of a little dark and heat. She moved forward.

"Kirsten?" She heard a noise, a soft meowing somewhere in front of her. "Maurice. Here boy, here. Kirsten, can you hear Maurice?"

Her hand snaked forward now, locating the path with some skill. Even though it was dark in the closet, her eyes had adjusted enough for her to make out distinct shadows. A light clicked on in front of her.

"Look what I found," Kirsten said, jiggling a flashlight in Jessica's face. "It's ancient, but the batteries work. And how about this?" She shone the flashlight on her head to show she was wearing a black metal helmet with a Civil Defense insignia on it. "Neat, huh? Let me show you what else is in here."

"Kirsten, why didn't you answer me before? I thought something happened to you."

"What could happen? It's just a big old closet filled with junk. Anyway, wait till you see what I found."

"You could have fainted in this heat. Giant rats could have attacked you. That's what might have happened."

"Okay, okay, I'm sorry I didn't answer. But take a look at this stuff." The flashlight beam swept across a row of olive green uniforms, each starchily neat and wrinkle free, each bearing insignias and stripes. "WAC uniforms," Kirsten said, fingering a cloth badge on the arm. "Real ones. Fifty years old and in perfect condition."

"Well, she's old enough to have been in that war," Jessica said.

"She's old enough to have been in the Revolutionary War," Kirsten said. "And look here."

Just past the army uniforms was a rack of long, dark business dresses with wide lapels. From a box on the floor, Kirsten produced a small hat. "Says 'Ridgewood Hatters, 1936' in here. 1936!" She put the hat on Jessica's head and pulled the net veil across her eyes. "Stunning, Jessie darling. Just stunning." She didn't wait for a reaction from Jessica, but pulled her along the path a few feet. "And get a load of these."

This time Kirsten was holding out a short, glittery dress with long fringe at the bottom. "It's roaring twenties time." She drew a long feather boa from the shoulders of another dress and wrapped it around herself. "How do I look?"

"Like a baldheaded bird." Jessica wiped sweat from her face. "It's too hot to mess around in here, Kirsten. Let's find Maurice and get out."

Kirsten pushed the Civil Defense helmet

up and used the boa to wipe her forehead. "I guess it is a little hot. But I still want to look around some. Let's go to the back of the closet, then you can find Maurice and I'll go through some boxes. I'll lead the way."

What else is new, Jessica thought, trailing after Kirsten. The many angles in the path made walking slow and Jessica found she had to step over boxes and shoes more often.

"More uniforms," Kirsten said in a hot, weary voice. "World War I, I think."

"Probably," Jessica said. "Don't you think this closet is awfully big?"

"I guess." Kirsten pushed past a frilly dress loaded with petticoats that Jessica recognized as turn of the century vintage. "Probably runs the length of the house."

"What?"

"The closet. It probably runs the length of the house, from one side to the other. Maybe it's just a big room and she's loaded it up with clothes over the years. Kinda dumb, if you ask me, but what do you expect from somebody who saves everything."

"I'm not sure all this is hers." Jessica held up a pair of worn riding boots. "These look ancient."

"Look at this," Kirsten said, handing a brass button to Jessica and shining the light on it. "I stepped on it."

"There are letters on it. Says 'CSA.' 'CSA?'" Jessica repeated the letters several times, rolling them inside her mouth.

"Consolidated Shoppers of America." Kirsten laughed at her own joke. "Get it? She has all of this stuff. . . ."

"No, listen," Jessica blurted out. "CSA — Confederate States of America. We're in the Civil War clothes."

"Civil War!" Kirsten whisked the button out of Jessica's hand, scrutinized it carefully, then popped it into her pocket with the cat's-eye. "Do you see the uniform it came from?" She was already pushing clothes aside, poking shafts of light everywhere in a frenzied search. "I can't find it in this mess. I know, we'll go to the back and then really search this area when we come out. See if you can remember where we are, okay?"

"It's like we're in some kind of time machine," Jessica said, her voice a shaky whisper. "Every step we take moves us farther and farther back in time. Next it'll be the War of 1812. Then . . ."

"Jessica, get real, will you? We're in an old lady's closet that's loaded with clothes and shoes and boots and a button or two." Kirsten aimed the light directly at Jessica's eyes. "Time machines are science fiction and that's all. You read about them, you don't walk into them."

"But don't you feel it? The way the dresses are closing in on us, making us move forward. . . ."

"Hey, don't go all weird on me. We've

still got a lot of exploring to do."

"I'm not sure we should," Jessica said. "Let's go back before . . . before . . ."

"Before what? Before it's too late?" Kirsten's mocking tone had returned. "Anyway, what about little Maurice? You were the one who wanted to find him. Or do you want to leave him in the time machine with the evil dresses?"

"It's not funny, Kirsten. Something's going on here, something strange. For all we know, Maurice might even be a part of it. We should go back."

"Oh, great. Now a cat has lured us into a time machine." Kirsten sounded angry. "Look, you can go back if you want. I'm going to do some exploring." She turned and disappeared into the wall of clothes.

Darkness was the first thing Jessica noticed. Total black darkness. And aside from Kirsten's shoving dresses aside just ahead, there wasn't a sound. So much for my good friend status, Jessica thought. It felt nice while it lasted. Maybe all the talk about the time machine *was* too much.

Jessica began searching behind her for the path that would lead her to light and cool, fresh air. She'd deal with Kirsten later, she decided. Maybe she'd be calmed down after she'd found a few more treasures. But where was the path?

The path had disappeared, consumed by the frilly petticoats, dresses, jackets, and coats.

Jessica pushed aside the clothes, but was greeted by another wall of them. And another and another.

It's just a closet full of old clothes, Jessica told herself very deliberately. Nothing more. And if I walk directly back toward the door I'll find my way out. Only she wasn't sure which direction led to the door. The zigzagging path had disoriented her enough that she could be headed toward one or the other side walls. There was no telling in this space since she hadn't seen the walls at all. Then she looked up and gasped. Above her, clear and sharp, was a night sky filled with stars.

"Oh, God," she whispered. Her hands had dropped to her sides, but she was still staring up at the twinkling lights. "It can't be. It can't."

This kind of stuff happened in those terrible movies, not in Mrs. Hayword's closet.

She moved her body slightly and brushed against a dress. Pulling away from its touch, she hit another and spun, her arms flailing against fabric but never escaping it.

"Kirsten!" she screamed. "Kirsten!"

"What now?" came the reply.

Jessica bolted toward the voice, located the path, and was with Kirsten a few steps later. "Look up," she said between pants of breath. "At the ceiling. There are stars above us. A closet with a sky and stars."

Kirsten gave the ceiling a fleeting glance,

then leveled a cold look on Jessica. "What are
you talking about?"

"Look at it. How can you deny it's the
sky?"

"She's poor, you said so yourself. She
hasn't had the roof fixed in years, so now the
roof has holes in it and so does the closet and
so does your head. End of story."

"Kirsten . . ."

"End of story." Kirsten headed toward the
source of the breeze. "I'm really disappointed
in you, Jessica. I thought you might be cool,
you might fit in. But you can't even walk
through a closet without freaking out. . . ."

Jessica mumbled quietly as she followed
along like a little kid, her eyes fixed on the floor
in humiliation. She brushed past more clothes,
older than any of the others and with a home-
spun quality about them, but Jessica hardly noticed. She's right. I freaked out. Completely.

The air grew steadily cooler and Jessica
thought she even felt a breeze brushing her
cheek. Next, something crunched underfoot. It
didn't take long for her to realize she'd stepped
on a leaf. A bunch of leaves really. The floor
was covered with them. The dresses here were
plain, like those worn by early settlers.

Suddenly, Kirsten stopped walking.

"Jessica," Kirsten said. The tone of her
voice had changed drastically, become hushed
and shaky. "Look."

When Jessica looked up she saw that the

clothes had disappeared in front of them. Only there was no closet wall either. Instead, they had stepped into a forest. A real one filled with tall trees, shrubs, and rocks. Jessica checked behind her. The clothes had disappeared, too. They had stepped from the closet and entered a small clearing in a nighttime forest.

"What's going on?" Kirsten asked.

"I told you," Jessica said in a whisper.

Just then Maurice wandered into the clearing directly across from them. He sat at the edge of the trees and meowed several times.

Kirsten shined the light into Maurice's eyes. They glowed an eerie, deep green. "You useless bag of bones," she spit out. "I should have . . ."

The words stuck in her mouth as the forest came alive with dots of flickering golden light. Torches, Jessica realized. She looked around and discovered they were surrounded by torches, hundreds of them in a circle that was moving in on them.

"We've got to run," Kirsten said, but wherever she turned she found a torch blocking her way. "Do something, you idiot. We've got to get out."

"I told you, but you wouldn't listen," Jessica repeated. "It's no use."

"Can't you see what's happening? We're surrounded. We have to get out of here. We can escape if we try together."

"To where?" Jessica asked. "The closet's gone!"

Figures began entering the clearing, all of them wearing long, draping cloaks with hoods. In the sputtering torch light, the facial features were distorted and skeletal, sharply angled with deep-set eyes and stern expressions. Jessica felt herself growing weak-kneed. This is what kids felt like who were kidnapped and about to be tortured and killed. Death had a shape, a form, and it was inescapable.

"Who are you?" Kirsten screamed. "What do you want?"

"You've done well, Eugenia," a woman said. "Two of them this time."

"Only one interests us," came another woman's reply. Jessica felt her skin crawl. She knew that voice. The woman stepped forward and pushed the hood from her face.

"Mrs. Hayword!" Jessica said.

"You can't do this to me," Kirsten yelled. "My father's important. He'll get you. He'll get you all. You better listen to me."

Ignoring her, Mrs. Hayword stepped up to Kirsten and held out her hand, palm up.

"What do you want?" Kirsten screamed. "I don't have anything of yours."

The hand did not waver.

"I told you, I don't . . ." Kirsten began sniffing back tears. Standing there in the torch light, Civil Defense helmet tilted back, boa hanging limply from her shoulder, Kirsten looked even more pathetic than she sounded. "I don't . . ." Her voice faltered and then she fell silent. The next moment, Kirsten produced the Confederate button and dropped it into Mrs. Hayword's hand.

"Mrs. Hayword," Jessica said. "We didn't mean any harm. We were just trying to . . . you know, find something to do. Maurice went into the closet so we followed him."

"I know, Jessica," Mrs. Hayword said, still looking at Kirsten. "We all face temptations and some of us give in to them." She inched her hand forward and wiggled her fingers ever so slightly.

Kirsten studied the hand, then lowered her eyes. "I . . . I . . ." — she dug into her pocket and dropped the cat's-eye into Mrs. Hayword's hand — "I wasn't going to keep it. I was going to give it back."

"I'm sure," Mrs. Hayword said.

"I was," Kirsten protested loudly, pointing an accusing finger at Jessica. "I was, but she said I should take it. She's as much to blame as me. Ask her. Go ahead."

"I sort of am to blame," Jessica said, but Mrs. Hayword shook her head solemnly.

"You were a follower, Jessica, like most people. That doesn't make you innocent, not by any means. But if there were no leaders" — and here she glared at Kirsten — "if there were no leaders, there would be no followers. That's how evil is born."

Jessica hadn't noticed the hooded figures glide up behind Kirsten. At the moment Mrs. Hayword finished her sentence, the figures grabbed Kirsten's arms.

"Help me! Help me!" With every word, Kirsten struggled to free her arms, her legs flailing wildly in the air. The flashlight fell to the ground, shattering its glass lens. "Jessie! Jessie! Do something. You have to help me."

Jessica took a step toward Kirsten, not knowing what she should do. Before she had a chance to defend herself, her arms were seized and Mrs. Hayword positioned herself so she couldn't see Kirsten at all.

"Forget her," Mrs. Hayword said. "She isn't worth your caring."

"But she's my friend. She's only here because I asked her to help me watch your cats."

"She never was your friend and never would have been. People like her only use other people." Mrs. Hayword put both hands on Jessica's shoulders and a soothing reassurance took hold of the girl. "You're safe now, Jessica."

"But Kirsten," Jessica said. "What are you going to do to her?"

"Something good. Something to spare her and the world the meanness she possesses. Believe me, she will feel no pain. None whatsoever. And when we're finished she will be rid of her evil forever."

As Kirsten's terrified screams filled the clearing in the forest, Jessica felt herself growing detached from the scene, almost as if she were backing out of the clearing. She moved farther and farther away from the action and realized something for the first time. They're witches, she thought. Then darkness filled Jessica's eyes and she saw and heard nothing else.

A glass clinked gently before Jessica saw or sensed anything else. Her eyes opened and Mrs. Hayword was leaning toward her.

"I said, would you like some more water, dear?" Mrs. Hayword's smile was friendly and reassuring.

Jessica looked at her empty glass. How did I get here, she wondered. She didn't recall getting or drinking the water. In fact, she didn't remember anything much about the day. "Ah, no thanks," she mumbled.

She glanced around the room. Yes, she remembered the room and the furniture and the cats lounging all around. That much was familiar. And the cat-sitting job. The cloud in her mind began to lift. She and Kirsten were supposed to watch the cats. . . . Kirsten. Suddenly, from deep within, she heard Kirsten's last screams for help, screams aimed directly at her. She looked at Mrs. Hayword.

"It happened, Jessica. Eventually, you will remember it all and accept it."

"Where is she?" Jessica asked. She pulled away from the old woman, though she felt no real alarm. It was as if she'd been given a drug that neutralized her emotions. "I'll never accept it, I'll never understand."

"You will, Jessica. Trust me, you will." Maurice jumped up onto the couch next to Mrs. Hayword and nuzzled her arm. Mrs. Hayword's hooded robe was gone, replaced by a flower print dress with a white lace collar. All the soft innocence of a past age. "Jessica will understand, won't she, Maurice?" Maurice looked up at his mistress. "See, Maurice agrees, and he should know."

"But you're a witch," Jessica said.

"Witches are like everybody else. All shapes and sizes and kinds. You happened to bump into the good kind."

"But they'll miss her. Her parents and friends and . . . and . . ."

"Of course, for a time. And the police will come around with lots of questions, too."

And I'll tell them everything, Jessica thought. I'll show them . . . And here she blurted out, "The closet."

Mrs. Hayword smiled faintly. "And that's all they'll find. A small closet with a rack of clothes and nothing more. Nothing."

"But they'll find . . ." Her voice dropped off then, unable to say the name.

"Kirsten?" Mrs. Hayword suggested. "I'm afraid not. Another runaway, they'll call her. A sad case, indeed. There are witnesses who saw you two leave here, and witnesses who saw her at the train station. Good, reputable citizens, old and young. Some of your schoolmates, too."

Jessica's eyes narrowed. "Witnesses?"

"There are a lot of us around," Mrs. Hayword explained. "In schools, in government, in the police department, everywhere. You'll come to appreciate our numbers in time as well. So feel free to tell anyone and everyone your story. I doubt if they'll believe you. They might even think you had something to do with her disappearance."

Jessica felt as if she'd been lured into a room that had no doors or windows. She knew that the truth was just beyond the walls, just inches away, but there was no real way to get other people to touch or even see it. Her story sounded fantastic even to her, and she'd experienced it. Imagine what other people would say when she mentioned a never-ending closet filled with clothes that led her and Kirsten to a pack of eighteenth-century witches.

"Don't feel bad about it, Jessica. Kirsten *wasn't* a very nice girl. It wasn't in her to be. And to allow her to grow up and develop those skills, to learn how to manipulate hundreds, maybe even thousands of people so that they believe in her and let her run their lives . . . well, we couldn't let that happen. Too many people might be hurt. No, we're all better off without Kirsten — the one we knew, that is."

Jessica couldn't make eye contact with the old woman, so she searched the floor for a cat and studied it for a few moments.

"Let yourself be honest," Mrs. Hayword added. "If you could stop a river from flooding a town, you'd do it, wouldn't you? If you could stop a malignant tumor from spreading, you'd do that, too. And wouldn't the world have been better off if someone had stopped Hitler before he seized power?"

"But Kirsten wasn't like him. She wasn't very nice, but she never murdered anyone."

"In her heart she had. Her heart was as black as the night. We . . . my friends and I . . . we can see these things before you. We can't stop every one of them, but we do try to spare the world as much evil as we can."

Eliminate evil before it has a chance to do evil, Jessica thought. That was like finding people guilty and sentencing them before they actually committed a crime. It didn't seem fair, and yet she had felt the sharp slap of Kirsten's words and they had hurt as much as any fist. Kirsten was capable of doing bad things, had, in fact, led others to do them, too.

"Don't you think that's a good thing to do?"

"I don't know," Jessica whispered. "Maybe." This is too confusing, Jessica thought. It made sense, but something still didn't seem right. Jessica looked at Mrs. Hayword. "What happened to Kirsten?"

"Oh, she's right inside having a snack. Kirsten," Mrs. Hayword called. "Kirsten."

Jessica heard the tread first, light and

quick and self-assured. Next came the clicking of nails on the wooden floor. A kitten entered the living room and leaped up onto the couch, gently pushing Maurice's head to the side so it could get its ears rubbed. "Jessica, I'd like you to meet Kirsten. The good part of her, that is."

"Good part?" Jessica questioned. All of the other cats came into the room and sat on the rug, watching Jessica carefully.

"Yes, the good part." Mrs. Hayword opened an end table drawer and searched through a small pile of marbles until she found the right one. "And here is the bad part of her." Mrs. Hayword gave it to Jessica. It was a dazzling cat's-eye marble with a deep blue center that looked exactly like Kirsten's eyes. "You can take it home if you'd like to start your own collection. It's quite harmless now."

DEEP INTO IT

Alan Allan always was long-winded, but I guess he meant well enough. And I have to admit that when I looked up from the letter everything around me looked different, less mean and dirty and annoying. Even the muddy Coosawhatchie. Then I saw the tiny P.S. he'd stuck on the back of the last page: "Digger, when you get to Hendry County, Florida, ask for Miriam." That's all it said.

Now, I thought that had to be the dumbest thing anyone anywhere had ever written, and I almost went all the way back to New Jersey to tell Alan Allan so in person. I hadn't planned to go to Florida and I didn't know where any Hendry County was anyway. And how am I supposed to find someone named Miriam without her last name or her address. Think about it. I wander into this county and say to the first person I meet: "Excuse me, can you tell me where Miriam lives?" Jeez, they lock people away in padded cells for less. But then I figured that somehow he had known about South Carolina and the flies, so maybe he knew something about what would happen to me in Florida, too.

Too spooky, if you ask me. I didn't want to find out what Alan Allan might already know, so I swore then and there, with the Coosawhatchie as witness, that I'd never go to Florida. Ever.

I left South Carolina and got lucky real quick in a tiny town in Georgia named Santa Claus. Yep, that's its name. Kinda dumb, I think, unless of course you're a little kid. But dumb or not, the local cemetery needed a digger, so I took the job.

I stayed there two or three years before I had to move on. Wasn't anything specific made me leave, you know. Just this feeling deep inside that I had to go. Oh, there was these dogs that started hanging around whenever the full moon appeared, making noise and being pesky. Reminded me a little of Alan Allan's dog stories and made me wonder, if you know what I mean. I even tried to call Alan Allan to see what he thought about the dogs and ask him what he meant about Hendry County, but he'd left Holy Conception Cemetery and no one knew where he was. All I know is that I left on a Tuesday and had another job on Thursday in another Georgia town called Attapulgus, about four miles from Florida.

Nice place, too. I liked the town and the cemetery, and since almost everyone I have to deal with is dead, I liked the people, too. But after five years, I started to feel this tugging on my elbow again, this time urging me to go to Florida. The dogs were back, too, running through the cemetery, howling. Woke me up a few times. Naturally, I kept shrugging all of these things off. Then I started to have nightmares about Florida.

Strange, huh? Most people have nightmares about falling off buildings or being chased by psycho killers with electric Ginsu knives. Me, I kept seeing this giant map of Florida floating above me, while a bunch of dogs howled in the background. I told you it was strange. I didn't get much sleep for almost two months either.

I started worrying that maybe the day near the Coosawhatchie wasn't the worst day of my life and that the dogs might be those "dark and dangerous forces" Alan Allan had warned me about. Then I figured it was all bunk, start to finish, and that my brain was only trying to get me to see Florida. I decided I'd go to Florida and be done with it, so I could get a good night's sleep again.

I made another decision, too. Since I was going to go to Florida, I figured I might as well go all the way, so I took a bus to the biggest town in Hendry County, a place called La Belle. No, I didn't get off the bus and ask the first person I met where Miriam lived. I strolled around La Belle instead, seeing what the place and the people looked like.

I wandered up and down streets for two or three days. Then one afternoon, I was on a little back street when I spotted this old man sitting in a rocking chair on his front porch. As I got closer to his house, I saw that his skin had a tanned, leathery look to it and his face was a mass of wrinkles, probably from working outdoors all of his life. I remember telling myself that most likely I'd end up looking a lot like him.

That was when I got this feeling that I ought to talk to him. Now, to be honest, I didn't really want to find out any more about this man. I've always felt that being led around by your feelings can get you in a lot of trouble. But instead of turning around, I headed right up his walk and said hello.

He was friendly enough, but I can't say he talked up a storm. He was missing a lot of teeth, which made his southern accent double thick. I had to strain to figure out what he was saying. Right away, he told me his name was August J. Miller and he would be ninety-four years old in the spring and that he'd worked in the sugar cane fields before he'd retired. After he told me what working in the sugar cane was like, his conversation dried up like his skin. Mostly he rocked back and forth and nodded yes and no to what I said about the weather, the city, and the neighborhood. I'm no big talker, either, so after a few minutes I realized I was running out of chitchat. I started to get nervous and wondered what I was doing there and what he was thinking of me. Which is when I asked him if he knew Miriam.

Old August stopped rocking, leaned forward, and looked me up and down a couple of times. "Miriam, you say?"

I nodded.

August got this faraway look in his eyes. I shifted in my chair some and then August looked at me again.

"Miriam," he said again. "Haven't thought on her in years. Why, I guess Miriam's in the sloo like always."

"You know this Miriam?" I asked.

" 'Course. Everybody know Miriam. 'Cept outsiders."

I asked him where the sloo was and August waved a hand in the air. "Down that way. Twenty, thirty mile. Maybe more. Never really measured it myself. Keep askin' and you'll get there. Everybody know Miriam Bunnell. Everybody."

Which turned out to be true. I started asking about the sloo and Miriam Bunnell and it wasn't long before I had directions. The sloo turned out to be the Okaloacoochee Slough, this massive hollow of deep, stinking mud well south of La Belle, and Miriam happened to own about twelve thousand acres of that mud. Miriam also happened to own the biggest cemetery in the area, which was called the Miriam Bunnell Cemetery.

The next thing I know I'm talking to Miriam Bunnell in person. She was a big woman, over six feet four inches tall, and she loved to talk. Probably making up for all the words old August didn't use. The second I saw her she started telling me all about herself, where she grew up, how she came to own so much of The Slough, what her life was like, and so forth and so on, etc., etc. In fact, it might have been a half hour before I could work in mention of Alan Allan. The second I did she said, "Well, why didn't you say so before. I guess you'll be lookin' for work in The Yard."

The Yard is how she always referred to the cemetery even though it was a pretty big yard. I said I could use work and started to tell her what jobs I'd had in the past. "Don't matter," she said before I'd gotten much into my work experience. "If Alan Allan sent you to me you must know what you're doing. Come on, let me show you how this all works." So she hired me on the spot to run the Miriam Bunnell Cemetery.

Like I said, The Slough was this big, muddy mess, but that didn't mean there wasn't some regular dirt on it in places, or that it was flat and barren land. There was plenty of big trees, cedars mostly, dripping with vines, and lots of sticker bushes and swamp grass and giant ferns. The cemetery was on the most solid part of it. Maybe "solid" isn't the right word. You could walk on it and not sink out of sight, but it was still pretty spongy stuff.

I took charge of the cemetery the same day Miriam hired me, but it took a while to get used to the place. For instance, we never really dug a grave. You couldn't. After you started a hole it would flood with foul smelling black water, so you'd be waist deep in it pretty quick and the mud would be tugging your shoes and you under. To bury somebody, we'd start the day before the burial by cutting a big rectangle of grass from the top of the soil and then lay the cement liner for the grave in the rectangle. By morning, the liner would have sunk underwater and out of sight. On the day of the actual funeral, we'd wait till all the family and friends had gone home, then we'd put the coffin in and top it with the cement liner cover. Both would sink and eventually meet up with the liner down under. Then we'd shovel in dirt we brought in from drier places. It wasn't like digging a regular grave, and I missed that. But there was something fitting, regal even, about the way the coffin slowly sunk into the earth.

I also made my rounds every night, making sure everything was all right and thinking about what we had to do the next day. Miriam noticed me coming in from one of my nightly tours and warned me not to do it anymore.

"There are things out there," she said. "Black snakes and alligators and bats."

I told her about my first job, where Clement Arnold blew himself up and how I'd managed to walk away from that once I woke up.

"I figure I must be lucky about cheating Mr. Death," I bragged.

"There are stories that tell of other things in The Slough." Miriam leaned in very close as if we were conspirators. Her voice dropped low. "Bad things live in there, they say. Not human. Not animal either. Bad things that stalk when the moon is perfectly round."

"I'll take my chances," I said, figuring that I'd spent most of my life living in cemeteries, so if there really were such creatures I would have bumped into one by this time. 'Course, I thought about the dogs and Alan Allan's stories, but I shrugged them all off.

"It's your funeral," Miriam answered without a trace of a smile.

So I continued making my rounds. And when the moon was full I went out of my way to take a very long time out there. I wasn't about to be frightened off by a bunch of silly stories. Speaking of stories, I heard the next one from one of my workers, a young kid named Billy. Billy said it happened in another part of The Slough, a part owned by the state and open to the public. Billy swore it was true, but then again, Billy also thought the Confederates really won the Civil War. For me, it don't matter whether this story is true or not since it says something mighty interesting about the stuff we carry around inside us. And I'm not talking about blood and guts either.

▲ 10 ▲
SOMETHING ALWAYS HAPPENS

The car's engine rumbled and shook, was silent a second, then spit out a jolting backfire and rumbled some more. The faltering engine was running so unevenly that Nick, lounging comfortably in the backseat, felt the shuddering in his bones. Here we go again, Nick thought. Something always happens when you hook up with these two.

"Let it coast in neutral," Mitch suggested, "and give it some gas."

"Jeez," Alan grumbled, hitting the steering wheel of his battered Toyota. "Now what?"

The car went over a hill, then picked up speed as it headed downward. Alan pushed in the clutch and stepped hard on the gas. The engine backfired again, then went into its death sputter. Now comes the comedy, Nick told himself. Mitch and Alan were like a match and gasoline. Put them together and sooner or later there would be an explosion.

"You're flooding it," Mitch yelled. "Ease up on the gas."

"You said give it gas, so I gave it gas," Alan shot back.

"You were supposed to pump it gently, idiot, not stomp on the gas."

"Now he tells me."

That was when the engine seemed to draw its final breath and expire, not with a resounding explosion of gas, but with a hollow-sounding belch through the exhaust pipe. The car was still plunging downhill, but now the only noises it made were the hum of tires on asphalt and the steady, slow swipe of the windshield wipers pushing aside the mist.

"See what you did?" Mitch said, shaking his head in disgust. "Now we'll never get to the party. Or the beer."

"What *I* did! I was just doing what you said I should do. You're the one who . . ."

"It's your junky car," Mitch told him. "And if you knew how to drive . . ."

"What are you talking about?" Alan had turned to face Mitch, and the car began to wander all over the road. "At least I have a license and don't have to beg rides all the time."

Friends had warned Nick about Mitch and Alan. It's not that they went out of their way to cause trouble. In fact, that was the last thing on their minds. But they always managed to blunder into one misadventure after another, and then argue at top volume about who was at fault. Most kids stayed clear of them, but not Nick. They made what would have been a safe and very boring suburban life in central Florida a little more interesting and unpredictable. Well, Nick thought. Guess I better play the peacemaker. As usual. "Hey, guys. Guys," Nick said, pulling his legs in and sitting up. "You're giving me a headache. And, Alan, watch the road before we have a head-on."

Alan yanked the wheel around and the car lurched back onto the right side of the road. When they came to a flat stretch of asphalt the car immediately began losing speed. Alan turned the ignition key and tried to pump life back into the engine, but all he got was a feeble click-click-click.

"Pull onto the shoulder," Nick told him. "Where that side road cuts in. See it?"

The car slid off the edge of the ashpalt and onto the gravel, the front wheels sliding on loose stone and bouncing into ruts. The springs squeaked in protest, the contents of the trunk — tire iron, spare tire, lug wrenches, and assorted tools — crashed around wildly like some strange metal salad. A few moments and thirty feet later, the car came to a complete stop. No one said a word for a long few seconds.

Then Alan asked, "What do we do now?"

"I'll tell you what you can do with this car," Mitch started to say. "You can . . ."

"*We* can look at the engine," Nick put in quickly, poking Mitch in the back of the shoulder. "If we get our act together we can still make the party."

They got out of the car, opened the hood, and stood there staring into the dark engine compartment.

"You have a flashlight?" Nick asked, and immediately regretted the question.

"Ah . . . I'll look, but I don't think so," Alan said, ducking back into the car's interior and rooting around under the seats.

"Check the trunk, too," Nick suggested.

"No flashlight," Mitch said in disgust. "Can you believe this?"

"Mitch . . . Mitch, lighten up, will you," Nick said.

"But he . . ."

"I know, Mitch, but arguing isn't going to get us any beer."

"Yeah, I guess."

For the first time, Nick had a chance to study the area where they'd stopped. Even in the gloom of a misty night he could see cedar trees lining the road that stretched out ahead, long strands of vines hanging from some branches. The air felt heavy and a rank odor filled his nostrils. They had come to a stop in the middle of The Slough, a vast piece of Florida State parkland that was all water and quicksand and rotting, befouled vegetation.

As if reading his mind, Mitch said, "Stinks around here, doesn't it? Like something died."

"Yeah," Nick answered faintly, suddenly

distracted. The weirdest feeling had come over him, a strange sense that someone was out there in The Slough watching them. And waiting.

"You okay?" Mitch asked.

Nick blinked himself alert. "Yeah, I'm okay," he said. "The stink must have gotten to me."

Alan came back a second later, his hands empty. "I guess I left it at home. Sorry."

"He's sorry," Mitch said. "Great."

"How was I supposed to know?"

"Okay, okay," Nick said, trying to head off the next round of bickering. "It's nobody's fault, see. Stuff happens. We have to come up with some kind of plan and quick, and maybe we can get this show rolling again." He had drawn his sentences out as much as possible, hoping his brain would snap back into focus and hit upon a brilliant idea while Mitch and Alan were distracted. "Let's see, we could . . ."

Mitch kicked hard at the front tire. "We could set this junk heap on fire and see if anyone notices."

"Hey, nobody said you had to come along."

"Like I said," Nick interrupted, his voice loud and firm. "We need a plan. A real one. Or we'll be standing here all night."

When he finished talking, he realized that both his friends had fallen quiet, their eyes searching the darkness around them.

"You hear that?" Alan asked. "That sound."

"Yeah," Mitch replied.

"Where?" Nick wanted to know. "I didn't hear anything."

"While you were talking . . ." Alan started to explain.

". . . there was a screech," Mitch continued. "From in there."

"Some kind of animal," Alan said. "A big one."

A shiver, cold and dark, ran up Nick's spine. So the feeling he'd had was real after all and not just the product of mist and imagination. "Look, how about we do this. I'll walk back up the road. There was a house back about a mile or so. Mitch, you go up the road and see what's there. Alan, you take this little road here. There might be a ranger station in there where you can make a call. What say we meet back here in forty-five minutes or an hour."

"What say we come up with another plan," Alan said. "I ain't going into The Slough, no way. Not after hearing that . . . that . . . whatever it was."

"It's your crummy car," Mitch pointed out. "You're the one that got us into this mess."

"If you're so brave," Alan challenged, "why don't you go? Or are you all mouth?"

"Hey, if it was my car I would . . ."

Nick slammed the hood down furiously, the crash startling both Alan and Mitch. "I'll go, okay?" he shouted, and he marched to the side road and turned up it, his feet crunching angrily on the gravel. The first thing he noticed was that it wasn't a road at all. More like a path, and one hardly used, judging by the weeds growing in the middle. Now I've done it, he thought. I'm walking right into it. And yet he had to admit there was something pleasantly exciting about it, too. The quickness of the decision, the way he'd charged off into the darkness. Before hanging around with Mitch and Alan he would have probably stayed on the road, safe and boring.

"Hey, Nick, sorry," Mitch called out from the road. "I didn't mean for you to go in there. See what you did? Now Nick's all mad at us."

"Me! You didn't hear me telling him to go in there, did you?"

The sound of their voices quickened the pace of his legs. Nobody made me come in here, Nick told himself. I wanted to. Just then, their voices came floating through the vegetation. "You should have just done what Nick said and not started whining," Mitch said. "You're always whining about something."

"I am not," Alan whined. "I didn't break the car."

Nick had to laugh, and he did, out loud. They were a show, which was one of the reasons he liked them. A regular comedy duo. "Shut up," Nick yelled without stopping or turning around, "and go look for help."

"I told you." Mitch's voice was distant and hard to hear now. "Do what Nick told you to do and try not to screw up like usual."

"Look who's talking. You're the one who . . ."

Nick went around a turn in the path and the voices were gone, blotted out by the tangle of leaves and branches. For the first time he was truly alone.

Fog rose up from the watery ooze and drifted across the road. He came to an impenetrable wall of it and had to stop. If something was waiting for him, this would be a perfect time for it to pounce. He was helpless. Instead, the fog gradually thinned to show him the path ahead.

The path was narrow, maybe eight feet wide, and had an irregular, twisting course. It was like some monster's tongue, wiggling out to receive him. Then the sensation of being watched came over him again. And it was close, too, just beyond the edge of the road in the goo and concealing foliage.

The Slough was famous for the strange things that had happened in it — people who had stepped off the designated paths and disappeared in seconds, sucked under by the mud, their bodies never recovered. And the murders. There had been many of them, each one bloody and horrid, and almost every one featuring some form of dismemberment. It was almost as if The Slough had an appetite and needed to feed from time to time.

Run, a small voice in his head said. Run back to the car. Don't be stupid. But he didn't run. Instead, he shook the cold feeling from his shoulders and went to the side of the path.

Go back and you might as well join the Future Lawyers Club and bore yourself to death. What you want is here, right in front of you.

He reached a hand toward a large, leafy bush, careful not to step off the solid path. It might be right here, he thought. Waiting.

He inhaled and held his breath, listening carefully. That was when he realized The Slough was absolutely quiet. No birds were calling, no animals scurrying in the dark. Even the insects had disappeared. He flicked his hand to the side almost as if he were slapping at the bush, and the leaves flew apart. All that waited for him was another layer of leaves.

"So much for hungry beasts," he said, releasing the air from his lungs in a gust.

He spent a few moments studying the area around the shrub, poking at branches with a stick he'd found on the side of the path. Nothing. Not even a mean-looking mosquito. When Nick continued walking up the path, his legs felt stronger, more confident. Every once in a while, he would jab at a wisp of fog with the stick, like a knight wielding his broadsword.

A light rain began to fall and the air grew clammy and raw. This is no fun, Nick thought, remembering the dry comfort of the Toyota's back seat. He would have gone back to it, too, except that at that very moment he spotted a pinprick of light up ahead. Nothing definite. Just a pale yellow glimmer.

A tiny spark of celebration bounced around inside Nick's head. It might be a ranger station or maybe a light over an emergency phone. Whatever, he'd been the one to find help and he'd done it pretty quickly, too. And it only happened because he had dared the wild noise and his feeling of being watched by entering The Slough.

Remember that, he told himself, tossing the stick into the darkness. Parents and teachers are always lecturing you on this and that, always trying to make you learn something. But he'd learned the most valuable lesson of all right here on a soggy, foggy little path: follow your instincts and then stick with it. Don't be spooked into running.

By this time, he'd moved close enough to the light to see that it was coming from a small window. Good, he thought. That means someone is probably there. We'll have the car going and be at the party in no time. He stopped on the path in front of the building, shivering against the cold rain.

It was definitely not a ranger station. More like some squatter's shack really — one story tall and covered with tarpaper, maybe twenty feet wide at most, with a sagging porch loosely attached to the front. He'd heard about the squatters, how the state had bought all the land back in the late forties for a park but had let the squatters stay on the land until they died or moved away. Then the bulldozers were brought in to level the shacks and outbuildings, and the wild plants would be allowed to take over again. One by one the squatters and all traces of them disappeared.

This must be one of the last ones, Nick thought. He noticed a thin vapor of smoke trailing from the black metal stovepipe. Smoke meant there was a fire, and that meant warmth.

He crossed the tiny dirt yard and bounded up the three steps to the porch, his running shoes thumping loudly on the worn floorboards. He was searching for the doorbell when a bolt clicked and the door squeaked open a sliver.

"Yes?" a woman asked suspiciously, her eye pressed close to the opening. "It's very late."

"Yeah, I know. Sorry," Nick said. The woman's voice sounded ancient. Even with the door open just a crack and no porch light on, Nick could see a thousand wrinkles radiating from the corners of her eyes. "Our car broke down and I wondered if I could use your phone to get help."

The woman's eyes swung from side to

side, checking beside and behind Nick. "There are others? You said 'our car' and that means there are others."

"My two friends," Nick explained, motioning with his hand up the winding path. "They're on the main road trying to get help. Can I use your phone?"

"You're alone, then?" The door opened wider to reveal a white-haired, frail-looking woman in a dark brown dress. She's got to be in her eighties, Nick thought. Late eighties at that. And the skin on her face and arms. It's pure white, as if blood hasn't reached it in years. The woman stood aside to let Nick enter, and a comforting warmth wrapped itself around Nick and drew him into the shack's main room. "Can't be too careful these days," the woman went on, " 'specially a woman at night. World is filled with strange people, strange things."

"Definitely," Nick answered, taking in the room at a glance. The room and everything in it was old, of course, and lit entirely by flickering oil lamps. But that wasn't what surprised him. The place was perfectly neat — every surface was dust free and polished, every pillow plumped and positioned just right, the curtains ironed.

"Have a seat," the woman said. "Name's Betty Ann Ralston, but hardly anyone calls me by my full name. Just Betty will do." She was pointing Nick toward a seat nearest the metal stove.

"Nick," Nick said. He didn't really want to sit down. He wanted to get help as quickly as possible. But the old woman was so eager for him to sit that he eased himself into the chair, a big, overstuffed thing that hugged Nick tightly. "That's my name. Can I use the phone?"

"No," she said firmly, then broke into a laugh. She sat on a straight-backed wooden chair on the other side of the stove opposite Nick. "Don't have one, you see. I would, but the phone people don't string wire in The Slough. Some sort of regulation. No 'lectricity either. Guess the state doesn't want us to get too comfortable out here." She laughed again. "Husband and I, we've been livin' here, oh, some forty years now, maybe more. Who counts? Imagine, all that time and never hearing a phone ring?"

Betty went on talking about forty years of living in The Slough and what it was like, but Nick had tuned her out, much like he tuned out Alan and Mitch. Now what, Nick wondered. He couldn't sit by the fire all night listening to some old lady reminiscing. He had to get moving, and soon, or the night would be a waste.

". . . There were more of us living in The Slough back then. Maybe twenty families and . . ."

"Excuse me," Nick said, leaning forward in his seat. "Do you know if there's a ranger station up the path? Or an emergency phone?"

"A ranger station?" She looked thoughtful a second, then shook her head. "No, no, can't say there is. 'Course, I've never been far into The Slough. Stay home most of the time, cleanin' and straightenin' and such. Leave the wandering to Henry. Henry's my husband. Been married . . ."

"Is there an emergency phone anywhere around? What do you do if someone's sick or gets hurt?"

"Emergency? Hmm, haven't thought much about that. In the old days, when folk still lived nearby, we went to one another in time of trouble. Edwina Lee — she was married to Hamp Lee, one of the sweetest fiddlers ever — anyways, Edwina brewed up potions to ease the pain, knock a fever down, put you to sleep. Owen Thrift knew how to set broken bones and pop dislocated arms back into sockets. Everybody had a specialty, you see. If a black widow spider got you, you went to Mizells', Iva and Tom, and they mixed up their herb mud to draw out the poison."

Can't she see I'm in a hurry? I told her I was looking for help. Nick placed his hands on the arms of the seat, ready to push himself up, but hesitated. Betty's eyes were alive and said she was enjoying his company. Even her skin had a rosy glow to it now. It seemed impolite to walk out on her. Give her a few minutes before leaving, he told himself. Let her talk a little and then. . . .

"Tea?"

"Huh?" Nick was so startled by the question that he fell back into the seat.

"Tea? Some tea might help take the chill from your bones." She had already gotten up and retrieved a black kettle from the floor next to the stove, shook it to make sure there was enough water in it, and placed it on the stove top to boil. "I make my own tea," Betty said, as she went to a tiny room that Nick assumed was the kitchen, "from bark and leaves and flowers. Edwina taught me how before she died."

"That's okay," Nick protested. "I have to be going. My friends are waiting." There was no response from the old woman, though she'd reentered the room carrying two white cups. "I'm supposed to be getting help. For our car."

"You've only just gotten here," she said. "And it won't take but a minute for the water to boil." She placed both cups on a foot stool and moved it so it sat between her and Nick. When Nick glanced into the cups, he saw a small pile of twigs, grass, and leaves in each one. "Just one cup?"

Debris was the word that flashed through Nick's mind when he saw the stuff in the cups. Swamp debris. But it was a tiny cup and he could probably choke it down in a minute or two. "Yeah, sure. A cup. But then I have to be going."

"Of course." The kettle whistled and

Betty poured steaming water into the cups. In-
stanly, the water turned a muddy black color.
She handed the cup to Nick, who took it with
two hands and held it in his lap. "As I was
saying, everyone helped everyone else with
emergencies. The same was true for everyday
things, too. The Presley brothers had a saw
blade and traction engine, so they cut boards
for us all. We built this cabin with boards from
them. Reeve Harper was the best tracker here
about. If you needed food, Reeve could scare
up any sort of creature inside of an hour." Betty
raised her cup to her lips and sipped the brew
delicately. "How's your tea?" she asked.

The steam had carried the tea's fumes to
Nick's nostrils. Rotting bark, decaying leaves,
muck. Those were the images that flashed
through Nick's mind as he raised the cup to his
lips and took a tentative sip. It tasted worse
than it smelled. "Hot," he said, and quickly
added, "but good."

Betty smiled and took another sip from
her cup, and Nick did the same, though this
time he drew in as much of the hot liquid as he
could. The liquid scalded his tongue and throat
as it went down, but Nick forced himself to not
react in any way. Get it over with, he told
himself.

"I was a weaver myself. Learned from my
mother. Made all of the cloth for our clothes,
for the curtains, you name it." She looked
around the cabin proudly. "Made cloth for

neighbors, too. Once I made the whitest cloth ever for Rhoda Spaulding's wedding dress. Oh, you should have seen it. Whiter than the whitest bone porcelain. She looked beautiful standing there in the sun. . . ."

Nick took another sip of tea. For some reason it didn't taste as vile as before. In fact, it had no real taste at all. Just hot water with little bits of stuff floating in it. Something else occurred to Nick. His mouth and throat no longer burned. Maybe this is one of Edwina's pain relieving brews, Nick thought.

"And Henry did his share, too. He's a hardworking man, Henry is. Why, one day, he and Reeve and a little feller from over in Collier County named Dover" — here she stopped talking, slapped her knee, and laughed so hard she nearly spilled her tea — "that was his name for real. Dover. Dover Vandercroft. Imagine such a fancy name for this skinny little thing of a man. Anyway, those three went looking for alligators. . . ."

Henry, Nick thought. He had assumed Henry was another long dead memory of Betty's, but she'd talked about him as if he were still alive. Maybe Henry has some tools they could use. And a flashlight.

"Henry," Nick said. The name came out of his mouth as a mumble, as if he'd been asleep for hours. He cleared his throat. "You mentioned Henry . . . um . . . is he around?"

"He's out now looking for tomorrow's

supper. That's what I mean about my Henry. He could have waited till morning and light, but he didn't. Said he felt a big creature near and didn't want to miss the opportunity."

Mention of a big creature reminded Nick of the animal scream Mitch and Alan had heard. "Yeah, my friends . . . they heard it . . . the animal." His words were slurred and halting. "I didn't hear . . . it. . . ."

Why did he feel so tired, Nick wondered. The stove was giving off a lot of heat and the seat was deep and very comfortable, but that didn't explain the trouble he was having getting his tongue to say the words in his head. What was in the tea anyway?

"Henry has good hunting ears. He can hear a sound miles off. And Old Reeve Harper taught Henry everything he knew about tracking before he died. Henry knows all the trails through The Slough, and all the tricks too. He can get an animal to walk into a trap and not even know it." Betty smiled at Nick and nodded her head proudly. "More tea?"

"Ah . . ." No other words came out, so Nick just shook his head back and forth several times. "Got to go." The cool, wet air outside would revive him, like a rejuvenating slap in the face. Holding his cup in one hand, he went to pull himself out of the seat with the other, but his fingers couldn't haul his body up. "Hot in here. Can't breathe."

"I hadn't noticed," Betty said. "Henry's

the one who's always feeling hot. 'Betty,' he'd say, 'that stove's cookin' me like an August sun,' and he'd go and sit on the porch no matter how cold or damp it was. Me, I like it cozy and all. The good Lord didn't set men and women down on an iceberg. No. Put them in the Garden of Eden with palm trees and oranges and such, so we're supposed to be warm. Least that's what I feel. But Henry . . ."

The sides of the seat seemed to squeeze Nick in place, enveloping him. He tried to wiggle his shoulders, but they hardly moved. Even his eyes seemed paralyzed, staring ahead at the wall opposite where a picture of Jesus hanging on the cross stared back at him mournfully. He was stuck in the seat, trapped really, and should have felt panicky, but he didn't. Maybe it was the numbing effect of the tea, or maybe it was the soothing way Betty was rambling on and on. His grandmother would talk about the old days like this when she was getting the Thanksgiving turkey ready for the oven.

I walked right in here, he thought. I followed the path, thought I was brave, and walked right in here. Never suspected a thing either. Some dithering old woman and her stories and her tea. Walked right in. Right in.

Betty said Henry's name again, and the tiniest jolt of energy went through Nick. This can't be a bad situation, Nick told himself. She's too nice. Too old. I'm just not feeling well. If I can just get out of here, find Mitch and Alan, get back to the road. "Henry," Nick managed to say, "Any tools . . . repair our car?"

"Tools? Car tools, you mean?" Nick couldn't turn his head to look at Betty, but he could tell that she'd leaned forward in her chair. "I don't think so. We've never owned a car and Henry never was one for machines and engines. That was something the Presley brothers were good at, but they're gone now fifteen, twenty years. Not that Henry wasn't good with his hands, he was. Everyone brought their kills here. That was Henry's skill, you know."

"Skill?" Nick asked softly.

Just then there was the sound of footsteps on the porch. Maybe it's Mitch or Alan, Nick thought. They'll get me out of here.

Betty crossed in front of Nick and went to the door. "Henry's skill?" Betty answered as she undid the bolt lock. "He was a butcher. Worked in a slaughterhouse near Brandenton before we moved here. Could clean and dress a carcass better than any man hereabouts." There was a squeak as the door was opened. "It's a real art, butchering is."

Nick's vision was beginning to tunnel, the sight at the sides blurring and darkening. Even so, he could tell that the figure filled the door, something neither Mitch nor Alan could do.

"We were just talking about you," Betty said.

The figure at the door grunted, then came toward Nick's seat, his boots clomping loudly.

"Two bags? You had a good night," Betty said.

"And easy, too," Henry answered. His voice was surprisingly pleasant sounding, not at all gruff or harsh. "They stood next to their car like rabbits. No fight really."

"That's nice," Betty said. "You're getting on in years, you know."

Henry grunted again, stopping briefly in front of Nick. Nick's vision had shrunk to a small circle, and he couldn't move his body or head at all. Still, he could see the two cloth bags Henry had slung over his shoulder, each bulging and heavy, each stained dark red with fresh blood. "And this one?" Henry asked.

"Oh, we've had a very pleasant chat," Betty said. "Haven't we, Nick?"

Pleasant? Nick thought. Oh, yes, very pleasant. Like talking to Grandma. He would have said the words, but his mouth no longer moved.

Henry moved away, toward the kitchen.

"And the car? Nick here said it was broken."

"Just a loose wire," Henry said from the other room. There was a sickening thump as first one, then the other bag was dropped to the floor. "Drove it into The Slough. Gone. Sank like all the others." Henry came back into the main room and took off his hunting jacket. "I'll finish up with them first," he told Betty. "Then I'll do him."

"Whatever," Betty said. Nick heard Henry clomp back into the kitchen.

He means me, Nick thought in a surprisingly calm tone. He had Mitch and Alan in those bags. Pieces of them anyway. I'm next. I should be wild now, should be screaming and yelling and panicky, but I'm not. The fire is so warm and this seat is very comfortable. It's like I always said. You hang around with Mitch and Alan, and something always happens.

Just then, Betty leaned over and her face filled what was left of Nick's shrinking field of vision. This close, her skin looked incredibly soft, her eyes deep with care. "I'll make you more tea, Nick," she said, an angelic smile lighting up her face. "One more cup and you won't feel a thing."

▲ 11 ▲

FOOTPRINTS IN
THE SNOW

I worked in The Yard a long time, long enough to see my face fill up with wrinkles and for my hair to fall out of the places where I wanted it and start growing in places where I didn't want it. Then one day, Miriam died.

It was sudden-like and shocked everybody, even me. She was out walking one night when this wild dog charged out of the shadows and bit into her arm. Yep, you heard right. A wild dog, one of those dark and dangerous forces Alan Allan had always been flapping his jaws about. A couple years back a dog showed up one night, howlin' and growlin' at me. Then another and another, until there was a regular pack of them living nearby. I'd even been bitten a couple of times while checking to see that everything was okay in The Yard. Drew blood, too. But I'd whop the beast with my shovel and it'd yelp and run off and that would be that. Didn't even bother going to the doctor. Any-

way, back to Miriam, her bite was bad enough,
but it wasn't the sort to carry off a life. So when
Miriam came back with her arm all bloody, I
didn't think much of it until she announced.
"I'm going to be gone soon, Digger, you hear?"

"Where are you going?" I asked and she
gave me a look that said she wanted to take my
shovel and hit me one in the head.

"To my eternal reward," she answered.

I told her the bite didn't look so bad, but
she wouldn't have none of it.

"I've felt it for a while," she said. She
didn't sound any different than before. She just
said this all matter-of-fact, as if it didn't really
mean much. "I knew my time was about up.
Known it for months. That's why I got work
started on The Box." The Box was her word
for the crypt she was having built for herself
close by the gates to The Yard where the
ground was real solid. "Now help me inside so
I can get ready, then call my boy so I can tell
him what to do after. Oh, and make sure those
flowers over by the fence get watered will you?"

I reminded her that I'd been bitten, even
showed her the scars, but she just shook her
head. "Some don't die. A few. The rest do, and
I'm one of them." Next she waved off my sug-
gestion that she see a doctor with "No use. Now
you listen. Won't be no one to watch over you
when you take those strolls at night, so you be
extra careful, especially when the moon is full."
I told her I would but I wasn't very convincing.

"Young fool," she said, shaking her head. "Bad things are out there, Digger. You've been lucky so far, but they're waiting. You take heed."

Miriam took to bed a little after her son arrived, talking every minute of the way, and by morning she was dead. Just like that. Her son, Jeff Davis Bunnell, came out and told us the news and added, "She didn't want any of you to be sad, see. And she wants to have a funeral people hereabouts will remember."

I think she got her wish there. Miriam's funeral was one of the best ever at The Yard. The Box was huge and gaudy, and it was almost finished, so Miriam could move right in. Thing had spires at every corner, carved gargoyles above the entrance way and wrought iron gates for doors. To liven it up, her son had red, white, and blue bunting wrapped all around it. It even had solar panels on the roof so that Miriam's favorite music could play twenty-four hours a day. It was a sight all right, like something you'd find at a carnival, and Miriam would have loved it. "I want to go out in style," Miriam had said more than once in the years I was there. And I guess you could call this style. Miriam's anyway.

Everybody knew about it, too. Newspapers in the county had run stories about The Box while it was being built. When they told about Miriam's death later, people from all over Hendry County came to see the funeral. Hundreds and hundreds of them. Which is ex-

actly what Miriam wanted. Fact, she had pro-
vided money for a big barbecue to be held the
day she was set in the ground. Imagine it. Grills
cooking up ribs and chicken, people wandering
all over the place with their food, and couples
dancing while The Box cranked out tunes. No
mistake about it, it was some lively funeral.

Miriam didn't want us to be sad and it was
pretty easy not to be while the funeral was in
swing. But when it finally ended a day or two
later, it really hit us. We missed Miriam and we
knew things just wouldn't be the same without
her. For one thing, it was awfully quiet, what
with Miriam not there talking morning to night.

Oh, Jeff Davis did his best. Didn't change
anything about the way we worked in The Yard
and let us alone for the most part. Miriam did
her part, too, what with The Box playing tunes
all the time. As for me, I did everything the
same as when Miriam was around even to taking
my walks at night.

Those wild dogs were still around. Even
bolder than when Miriam was here, it seemed.
Some nights you could see two or three of them
running through The Yard, chasing each other,
and yapping loudly. They were all big creatures,
bigger than any normal dog, with long legs,
huge feet, and shaggy gray coats. I could see
how Alan Allan might call 'em wolves, which,
of course, made me wonder if these were the
same animals he'd seen. Even when you didn't
actually see one, there was movement in the

woods, and glowing eyes peeking out of the darkness. Nights like that I'd walk right to where they were and even turn my back on them.

They came at me, of course, which is what I wanted. They'd come up and I'd give them a lick with the shovel, all the time thinking, "That one's for Miriam."

They got me a few times, in the hand and leg. One even took a nick out of my throat, which just made me madder. I wondered if one of these bites might carry me off like it did Miriam, but I never so much as got a headache. Well, if these were the dark and dangerous forces that were going to get me, they were doing a pretty feeble job of it.

Then one night, all the dogs came at me at once, growling and snarling and circling around me, dodging between the gravestones. It was hard to see them, the night was so murky. But I didn't budge an inch, just held my shovel ready for action. They circled me a while, stopped and growled at me, then circled in the other direction. It was like a dance or a ceremony. The next thing I knew, this dog appeared at the edge of The Slough, still deep in the shadows so all I saw was its eyes and teeth. It let out a growling howl, long and sad, and all of the other dogs ran off into The Slough. Vanished like the fog and never came back again. Bizarre. I looked up and saw a full moon in the sky.

Wasn't long after that Billy left to work

in the Everglades as a guide. Then two or three
others pulled out. I stayed for almost a year
after Miriam died, helping Jeff Davis keep The
Yard going and training new people. But things
had definitely changed.

After the funeral, people still came to see
and hear The Box. Pretty soon buses were
showing up and Jeff Davis started to charge
admission to get close to The Box and wander
around The Yard. Once a cemetery gets too
lively it isn't a cemetery anymore even if you're
still burying people. Takes all the pleasure out
of digging a hole, or in this case, sinking a coffin.
So I left and started traveling around the country, taking jobs wherever there was one to find.

Oh, there were still some real digging jobs
around, mostly in small towns. Found one in a
tiny Mississippi town called Hot Coffee. You
don't believe me, but it's true and you can look
it up, too. Stayed a few years, but then the
owner said he'd have to go to machines to save
money, so I left. Next stop was in Biggers, Ar-
kansas, then on up to Pocahontas, Missouri.
And on and on, from one town to another. I'd
be there a while, then have to move because of
the machines. Felt as if they were following me,
you know, taking my job away from me. Came
to hate them, too.

They weren't the only things following me
either. Just about everywhere I'd stop, those
wild dogs would show up eventually. At first I
wasn't sure these were the same dogs I'd met

down in The Slough. My eyes don't exactly work as well as they used to in the dark and, anyway, it didn't really matter much. There was something comforting about having these dogs around so I never really checked them out very closely. It was like always having a little part of The Slough nearby. These dogs weren't ever nasty either. They'd just bark and growl at me a few times, sorta to say hello, I guess. They always left when the leader howled for them. I never saw much of the leader, just his teeth and eyes.

This moving around went on for a lot of years and eventually I found myself back in Garrison, New York. Think about it. I spend most of my life digging holes all over the United States and wind up where I started.

Garrison had changed over the years. My parents were dead a long time and even their house had been torn down. That wasn't all. Rich people had begun buying up all the land and houses, so it wasn't the factory town I remembered. It was a summer place now and not very interesting. Even the cemetery had changed.

I remember the night I walked to the cemetery and discovered this. It was also the night I learned a new story.

It was snowing when I got to the cemetery and nearly eleven o'clock. The first change I discovered was that the front gates were locked tight. When I was here, they were for show only. I had to wander around the outside of the fence until I found a hole big enough to squeeze through.

Once inside, things felt better, more familiar. The snow on the ground actually made the shape of the gravestones stand out more clearly, and I could almost imagine Clement Arnold and me carrying our shovels and picks to the next job. Thinking of Clement made me want to visit him, so I began searching for his gravestone.

That's not very easy in the dark, especially since I hadn't been in this cemetery for almost fifty years. I followed the narrow road over a couple of hills and came upon the next change in the place. There it was, this big black shadow sitting off to the side of the road. No mistaking what it was. It was a backhoe, its long neck and scoop stretched out like some extinct dinosaur. Only I was the dinosaur now.

Anger boiled up inside me. It wasn't fair — not the way this body of mine had gotten old, or the way machines had replaced me. Not a bit. I spit at the backhoe, then marched off to find Clement's grave. Took about twenty minutes, but I found it in a hollow.

The snow had stopped falling by that time and the whole place had a peaceful coat of white crystals on it. Made me wish Clement were around to tell me I should use my head or something else smart. I didn't go and talk to Clement or anything like that. I'm not that kind. But I did think about the good times I had with Clement, and also about being up in Guilderland, and with Alan Allan and Miriam. Nothing sentimental or anything. Just some of the things we did and stories we swapped.

About then I noticed that the night had brightened and all of the gravestones were lined up nice and pretty. The clouds had thinned and a full moon was right overhead and so clear you could see the outlines of craters. The next second, I heard the panting of dogs.

I looked around and found that the pack of dogs was standing at the top of the hollow eyeing me. Only this time I didn't have anything to swat them with, so I felt like a lump of hamburger meat in a bowl.

The dogs didn't move for a long time and neither did I. Standing there above me, they looked even bigger than I remembered and their eyes, yellow in the moonlight, seemed to be burning. Then they began barking and running around. Every so often, one of them would come charging at me, only they never attacked me. Just ran past me and up to the other side of the hollow. After a while, I got the feeling they were just out having fun, that they weren't going to attack me, so I began to relax.

These must be the same dogs, I told myself. They look and act like the others, but why have they been following me for — how long has it been? — almost thirty years? How can any dog be that old? That was when the leader appeared and I saw him clearly for the first time.

He was gigantic, maybe one hundred and fifty pounds gigantic, and his coat was a deep, rich black color. He had powerful muscles in his chest, and you could tell he was the leader because all the other dogs stopped what they were doing to watch him. But that wasn't all. He only had three legs, his rear right leg being gone altogether.

"Alan Allan, is that you?" I shouted without thinking.

'Course, the black dog didn't answer. Instead, he growled and snarled and the rest of the dogs took off running, just like they had in the past.

I struggled up the incline, cursing my weary old legs all the way, and when I got to the top I saw them all disappearing over a ridge some two hundred yards away, the leader running as easily and quickly as if he had all four legs. Only this time, the leader stopped, raised his head toward the moon and gave out this long, mournful howl. What hairs were left on my head stood right up, it was such a scary sound.

The howling stopped and the black dog looked right at me. He howled again and it was then I realized I wasn't listening to a dog. He was a wolf, just like Alan Allan had always said. When the howling stopped again, the wolf looked at me one more time, almost as if it wanted me to follow, and then scampered off after its friends.

So there I was, standing in the snow in a cemetery with a lot of wolf prints leading off somewhere. So what did I do? I followed them.

Can't say I had a sane reason to do this. They hadn't tried to hurt me, so I didn't feel real scared. Maybe seeing that backhoe had something to do with it. Those machines had done more to annoy me in the past than the wolves, the few bites notwithstanding. And there was that black wolf, of course, one-legged like Alan Allan.

That thought got my attention. It was too silly to think that Alan Allan had somehow got turned into a wolf, but the notion stuck. Seemed to make as much sense as anything else, so I decided it could be true.

The snow was a few inches deep, so it was pretty easy to follow the paw prints through the cemetery and to the place where they'd gone through the fence. They went across the highway and into the backyards of some houses, and so did I. There were a lot of trees here, which made seeing the tracks real hard. Had to stop a lot to search the snow for them. Plus I was out of breath and my legs felt like they were made of cement.

About this time, I started to feel foolish. What was I going to say if someone stopped me and wanted to know why I was trespassing? A three-legged wolf who was once a human invited me to follow him and his pack?

My shoes were sopping wet and making a

squishy sound every time I took a step. Eventually, the prints led me into town where the houses were close together. It wouldn't be long before somebody spotted me and called the cops. I was about to give up and go home when I saw something on the sidewalk ahead. The wolves were waiting there for me, as if to say I couldn't give up yet. When they were certain I'd seen them, they sprinted off.

Can't say I was happy to see them run off again, but I picked up my old legs and tried to stay as close as I could. Sometimes, I was so exhausted I had to lean against a tree to stop my chest from pounding. Finally, the prints led to the center of town.

It was after midnight by this time. Not many people around, though a few were coming from the movie. A couple of cars slipping and sliding along the icy road. The wolves had gone right past the town hall and into the park, entered it through a great wall of shrubs.

I hesitated outside those shrubs. It was dark in there, pitch black. For all I knew, those wolves could be waiting in there for their next warm meal to walk in. But if they were looking for food, they could have had me easy back in the cemetery or in any of a dozen spots along the way. And why would Alan Allan want to hurt me? Because I read the story when it wasn't the worst day of my life? I held my breath and started pushing through the shrubs, all the time trying to see where the tracks went.

The shrubs gave way to a tangle of brush and trees, and it was impossible to see any paw prints at all. I just kept moving forward, taking the easiest route through the woods. Not far along, the trees ended and a wide-open field stretched out in front of me. The wolves were waiting there.

As I approached them, the wolves began trotting across the field. They were side by side, maybe seven feet apart, and their heads were hunched down and focused straight ahead, the black wolf a little ahead of the others. I looked across the field and saw that the wolves were headed straight for a young couple out walking on the path.

Probably just came from the movie, I thought. Decided to take a romantic stroll before heading home. I thought to yell to them, warn them about the wolves, but I didn't. Instead, I began running after the wolves.

I never was very fast, even when I had young legs. So I was surprised when I found myself gliding along effortlessly some twenty feet behind the wolves.

I glanced behind and saw my footprints leading away from the woods, side by side with the wolf tracks. I was amazed that I had covered several hundred feet in just a few moments and didn't feel winded at all. When I looked ahead, the couple was closer and still unaware that we were approaching.

It's odd how the mind works, especially a

real old one. Earlier in the cemetery, I'd felt pretty good, thought about some of the good times and people I'd met. Now I was thinking of the others — my father and his mean streaks, the businessmen who closed Prospect Hills to build houses, the way machines kept taking jobs away from me. I could taste the anger in my mouth, metallic and bitter. Everything that had ever annoyed me, big, little, and silly, seemed to flash through my mind, making my blood pump even more furiously. Even being old wasn't fair. I wanted revenge and I wanted it now, so I focused on the couple ahead. They were probably the sort to push an old coot like me aside so they could have an easy time of it.

Just then, the wolves separated, leaving room between them. I pulled up next to them easily. I wasn't even breathing hard and my legs felt strong and young again. Powerful even. We were flying along, and I could hear their panting as loud as a train charging through the night. Nothing could stop us, I thought. Nothing could stop me.

I stayed with the wolves stride for stride, each step eating up yards of territory and bringing us closer and closer to our prey. I glanced around again and was shocked by what I saw. Fifty feet back I saw a pile of old clothes in the snow and the abrupt end of my footprints. Wolf tracks were the only prints I could see after that. I had literally run out of my clothes and turned into a wolf.

Oddly enough, it felt completely natural. In fact, all I thought was, so this is why they'd followed me all these years. I'd been one of the few to survive their bites, like Miriam had said, and all they wanted was for me to want to join them.

When I turned toward the couple again, I realized that my sight had changed. I could see everything in the dark, including the man's gold watch and his four hundred dollar Italian shoes. I could smell what he'd eaten for dinner on his breath. I was hungry, too. What some people would call ferociously hungry. As if I'd never tasted food in my life. That was the moment the couple realized we were there and the man turned and opened his mouth to scream. But it was too late. I'd already launched myself at him, mouth open and fangs ready to tear the scream right out of his throat.

▲ 12 ▲

DIGGER'S GOOD-BYE

You didn't think I'd just up and leave without saying good-bye, did you? I wouldn't do that to you. Not after all we've been through together.

I can tell you're confused, wondering whether I'm an old man or a young wolf. The answer is I'm both, though right now I'm the old man, shaky hands and all. After the attack I followed Alan Allan — I was sure he was the three-legged wolf — and his pack throughout the rest of the night. I can't remember what we did since everything after the first attack is fuzzy. I do know that I woke up in bed the next morning my old human self. Well, maybe not exactly my old self.

I felt a lot better than usual, full of energy. My head was clear and not one muscle hurt either. When I checked myself out in the mirror I looked twenty or thirty years younger and a lot less weathered. That was some nightmare, I thought. Frightened the wrinkles right off my face. Then I saw my hands. There was dried blood under all of my fingernails.

One heck of a realistic dream, I told myself, and I sat right down on my bed to think
on it all. I discovered that thinking sometimes
doesn't help at all. No matter how I pieced
things together it always came out the same and
it always sounded too fantastic. I'd been a werewolf out hunting for food.

'Course, the next thing I did that morning was get a newspaper. There it was, big
as anything on the front page: "Couple Killed
by Wolves." The article was skimpy on de-
tails. Just told that the two had been mauled
badly, how many wolves were thought to be
involved, and how the bodies had been discovered.

I felt terrible, really terrible. Nearly threw
up at the thought of what I had done. Those
people hadn't done anything to me. They'd just
been in the park minding their own business
when we'd come along. It didn't take me long
to decide what I had to do — I walked down
to the police station to confess. When I got
there the place was crawling with all sorts of
people. State troopers, a posse of hunters and
trappers to track down the wolves, people
from the Federal Fish and Wildlife Department, and lots of regular citizens there to see
the action. Even the governor had come in by
helicopter, though I can't say I could see what
good he would do. Oh, and there were lots of

television reporters there, too. Those guys are worse than vampires when it comes to fresh blood.

As I said, I thought about turning myself in, but I decided against doing it that day. Naturally, I was worried that I'd be taken as an absolute certified A-number-one crackpot and locked away in some padded cell. Worse, I kept remembering something the sheriff had said in that newspaper article. "Rest assured," he promised the locals. "We are going to hunt those wolves down and destroy them as quickly as possible."

The word destroy put a real stop to my urge to confess. It sounded, well, nasty. A lot worse than kill or do away with or bring to justice. I mean, I felt bad, but I wasn't sure I was ready to go through a lot of pain just then. So I decided to let a few days slide by before confessing in the hope that the excitement might cool down some.

And I would have turned myself in except that something happened. I woke up the next day feeling stiff in the joints and headachy. The day after, my legs felt tired after walking a few blocks. A week or so later, the wrinkles returned. Not all at once, mind you. A few around the eyes one day, some more the next. Every day I woke up looking and feeling a little older. It wasn't long before I was back to my old decrepit self and not very happy.

You'd feel the same way if you saw and felt yourself aging three decades in the space of a few weeks.

I took to bed after this, too weary to do much else, least of all try to convince a lot of annoying people that I really did kill that couple. That's when the night terrors began.

Despite being in bed most of the time, I didn't really sleep much. Just lay there counting the cracks in the ceiling and thinking about that night in the park, about turning around and seeing where my footprints ended and where my wolf tracks took up. It was so clear in my mind, so sharp I could almost feel the power I had that night all over again. Nighttime was different. The sun would go down and my room would get darker, fill up with weird shadows and shapes. I knew better, but I was sure some of those shadows were alive and watching me. Once in a while, I'd drift off to sleep. Only I never had any dreams. Not even a good nightmare. I'd just close my eyes and enter this completely dark place. There wasn't a hint of light here, no sound. Nothing. It was completely black, like it must be inside a closed coffin. Then I'd think: maybe I really am dead. The second this thought came to me I'd wake up, my body shaking and sweaty.

Waking up once like this is pretty bad. But when you do this three or four times a night, three or four nights in a row, well, let's just say it doesn't put you in a peaceful frame of mind.

One night I woke up and felt even worse than usual. I was shaking all over, sweat dripping off my body and drenching the sheets. To clear my head, I got up and started pacing around my room. Walking hurt a lot, but that didn't stop me. Back and forth, back and forth. Only instead of getting rid of the edgy, bad feeling, it seemed to get worse. I passed near the window and noticed there was a full moon hanging up there in the sky.

People always feel strange when the moon is full, I reminded myself. Then I saw movement in the parking lot behind where I was staying, sleek shadows gliding silently through the dark. Alan Allan in wolf form stepped into the bright moonlight and stared up at my window. The other wolves were right behind him.

I have to admit I wasn't too sure what to do, so I started pacing again. Back and forth, back and forth. Every time I passed the window, they were down below, waiting. Urging me to join them.

I thought about the couple we'd killed and kept on pacing. I really didn't want to do that again. Then I remembered the way my legs carried me along, the way I had this unlimited energy, the way my senses were so sharp. Did Alan Allan feel the same? Did he and the others go from human to wolf form whenever the full moon was out? And would I feel better if I was a wolf again?

When I looked out the window the next time, Alan Allan was dancing around, his tail wagging wildly. He seemed to be signaling me, telling me to hurry up. I turned around and started across the room. Suddenly, a painful hunger started gnawing at me. It's perfectly natural, I told myself. Wolves have to hunt food like any other animal. And if that food happens to be humans . . .

The next second, I heard the clicking of nails on the floor of my room. My nails. I'd changed into a wolf again and all of the energy and power was back. It was scary how quick it happened. Think something positive about werewolves and, poof, you're one of them. But I guess that's the same with most other evil things. Once you start to see the slightest thing good about them you're hooked. And I was. For the first time in weeks I felt really good, really alive.

I looked at the window. My room was on the second floor, but it didn't matter. I had to get to the other wolves. I bounded across the room, leaped and crashed through the window, shards of glass flying all over the place. My landing was clumsy enough, but I managed it without breaking any bones. Then I joined the wolf pack, Alan Allan in the lead, as we sprinted off for a night of hunting.

I could tell you some fine stories about

being a werewolf, about stalking prey and changing back and forth and all that. But I can't right now. You see, the moon is beginning to rise in the night sky, big and bright and round. If I'm not mistaken, people refer to it as a hunter's moon. They don't know how right they are.